RANKIN: ENEMY OF THE STATE

JOHN OSIER

ST. LUKE'S PRESS
MEMPHIS

Library of Congress Cataloging in Publication Data
Osier, John, 1938 —
  Rankin: Enemy of the State

  1. Title.
PS3565.S55E6 1986 813'.54 85-27651
ISBN 0-918518-43-1

Book and jacket design by Susan Watters.

ST. LUKE'S PRESS
Memphis, Tennessee

For Wes with love.

Who's to doom when the judge himself is dragged to the bar?
Herman Melville

CHAPTER ONE

Rankin had been swimming for what seemed a long time, but in reality could have been no more than four or five minutes. He was numb with cold and already close to exhaustion. As he struggled toward the pier jutting out of the darkness, he was afraid the fierce current would sweep him past it. He thrashed harder. His arms felt like stone, his lungs ached. The end of the pier came close. He lunged for it and swallowed a mouthful of muddy river. Gasping, choking, he wrapped himself around the piling. He clung to it like a spent lover.

From up the river came the throb of a powerful engine. A pair of red running lights moved toward him: a searchlight beam knifed out and swept the bank. Rankin let go of the piling and, groping among others, found a ladder. Heaving himself up it, he collapsed on the rough planks face down.

The searchlight's beam played on the water, crept closer. He dragged himself along the planks and crawled behind a couple of large metal drums. The launch's engine grew louder and muffled his own thudding heart. Sudden as gunfire, light shot onto the drums, revealed vividly their leprous rust. One cheek pressed against the cold metal, he felt his whole body seem to contract and shrink from the light like a huge grub beneath an overturned log. The light probed along the pier toward the concrete revetment while the launch idled. At last it pulled away, dragging the light like a tail.

He watched it go, then limped to the bank. He crossed some cobblestones and a railroad track then started up a steep, grassy bank. At the top was a row of crumbling brick warehouses. A tiny alley led between two of them, and he groped down it a little way before he stopped, slumped against a wall, and caught his breath.

Below he saw headlights on the railroad track. A car bounced over the crossties: the headlights jolted up and down—then the car swerved onto the cobblestones he had crossed and stopped. The headlights of the car shone on the pier and a man got out. He walked onto the piers, pistol in one hand and his head bent. Suddenly he stooped down next to the empty drums and touched a spot with his free hand. He straightened abruptly and stared up the slope at the warehouses. Then he started back to the car.

Rankin knew he must have discovered a wet patch that betrayed the fact someone had climbed out of the river and hidden there in the past few minutes. Soon Sepos would be swarming over the whole area looking for him. He had to get away from the river.

He closed his eyes a moment and saw again the teacher as the laser shot through his body and out the other side. Rankin shivered.

Less than an hour ago he had been an average citizen working at a boring job he had held for several years. Now he was hiding in an alley, and his future, if he had any at all, had narrowed to one inescapable fact: from now on anyone he saw would be his potential killer. He could hardly grasp the notion, let alone believe it. He must be having a nightmare, and any minute he would surely awaken.

But the wet clothes pressing against his skin, his dripping hair, and the chill breeze making him shiver were real.

He opened his eyes.

The car turned around and switched a spotlight toward the bottom of the embankment. The beam began to creep up the grassy bank toward the warehouses—toward the mouth of the alley.

Rankin turned and fled. He had to find some place to hide where he could be safe. But he knew of no such place. And as he stumbled down the black alley, he had no idea where he was going.

CHAPTER TWO

He stumbled down the alley as though in a daze, part of his mind still trying to deny what had happened. But the image of the bloodless face in his flashlight beam remained clear. Almost instantly he had recognized the face. He had seen it often enough on TV the past few days, but seeing it before him in the flesh had been a profound shock. His thoughts had been on Peg moments before. The breeze off the river with the smell and feel of autumn had recalled a similar night when the two of them had parked by the river and made love for the first time. But that had been before the war.

He had gazed across the river at the low Arkansas shore in the moonlight, feeling a strange twist in his belly, then heard the noise behind him and swung the flashlight around in time to see the figure dodge behind a piling by the foot of the pier. He took the billy club from his belt and started toward the piling.

As he drew near, the man rose from behind it. He did not run. His eyes blinked against the light, but he stood his ground even though he had no weapon.

One swift crack to the side of his head and Rankin told himself his own constant, nagging hunger would be a thing of the past, because now he knew who the other was, saw the fear in the blinking eyes and also the resignation. Maybe it was the resignation or the fact that he was unarmed that caused Rankin to hesitate. Or maybe it was just the surprise.

The Mississippi slapped gently against the pilings and the two barges, black and empty, moored alongside the pier. A lean rat scampered past, close enough to be kicked had Rankin a mind.

"What are you going to do?" whispered the other, a school teacher the TV said. His teeth suddenly begin to chatter. Sweat beaded on his forehead. It was not just fear, Rankin realized. The man was also sick.

Rankin flicked off the light.

He looked a pitiful specimen to be an enemy of the state, Rankin thought.

"What are you going to do?" the man repeated, then abruptly sat down along the edge of the pier.

"What's wrong?" The absurdity of the words overwhelmed him as soon as he spoke them. It was like asking a drowning man how he felt.

The other seemed not to notice. "I drank out of an old cistern last night, " he said tonelessly. "The water was bad. "

Rankin gazed down at him in uneasy fascination.

The authorities and half the population of Memphis perhaps were looking for the teacher and had been during the last five days, his face burned in their memories by the electronic tube, along with soap opera stars and cartoon characters and game show hosts. On the tube he seemed as big as them, bigger than life but, sitting before Rankin, he looked very ordinary, almost insignificant really with his shabby clothes and drawn, pinched features. Only the pallor of his face was at all remarkable, the result of his sickness.

Suddenly Rankin took his gaze from the man and looked around him. He saw no one in the dimly lit street that lay beyond the chained gate of the barge terminal. Since his clothes were dry, the teacher must have scaled the twelve-foot fence. Sick as he seemed, it could not have been easy.

Although Rankin could see nobody in the street, a stab of fear went through him. Somebody could be hidden and watching.

Why here? he wondered. Why in God's name had the teacher come here?

The man's teeth showed faintly as though he read Rankin's thoughts.

"A boat. I need a boat. "

"There's no boat here. " But it made sense. With a row boat, even if a man were too weak to row, he could drift down river in the dark and possibly elude the river patrols. Rankin glanced toward the street again. Each second that he delayed in calling the Sepos put him in more danger. He gripped the billy tighter and, for a moment, the teacher's eyes flicked toward the club.

"If you're going to do it, get it over with, " he said.

They claimed on the wallscreens that he was a subversive, an enemy agent. That was what they always said, but Rankin had always felt curious to know more—what they had really done. The question sprang to his lips.

He realized now, limping down the black alleyway, that asking the question had been the turning point. If he had not asked, if he had cracked the man with the club instead and telephoned the Security Police, he would not be fleeing for his own life at this moment.

The bitter hindsight gave him no satisfaction.

He reached the end of the alley and looked back. A few stars gleamed coldly out over the river. For the moment no one was behind him. He peered out into the street ahead. Except for the small islands of light around the few, scattered streetlamps, the street was nearly as dark as the alley. Silently he merged into the shadows and began to hurry down the street.

Most of the buildings along Front Street used to house the offices of cotton brokers—the street had been called Cotton Row—but now they were deserted and boarded up. He came to a streetlight and one window that was not boarded up. In the glass he glimpsed his reflection and except for his limp, he thought he looked almost exactly like the school teacher with the same shrinking air, shoulders hunched as though to make himself smaller, less visible—in fact, invisible, and the same ghostly pallor.

What did you do?

The teacher had told him. It was so dumb Rankin had almost laughed, doubting that could be all of it. The teacher had mimeographed copies of the Bill of Rights he said and plastered them up around the city in the dead of night.

"None of my students had ever heard of the Bill of Rights. I couldn't mention it in the classroom. It was the only way I could think of. I had a copy but destroyed it right after the war. " He gazed up at Rankin. "I wrote it from memory—after seven years. I'm not sure I got it exactly right. "

Rankin looked away from him at a tree limb floating past the pier. It went by swiftly in the strong current. The teacher had to be crazy. If he wanted to paste up a dead piece of paper and die for it, then he had to be crazy. His own choice was simple. He could kill the man for the full reward, turn him in for half, or else pretend he had never seen him.

"All those years I had lied to my students, " the teacher said. "All those years. Do you understand?"

Rankin shook his head impatiently. He did not understand.

A student had seen him pasting up a copy on a wooden fence like a circus poster, the teacher said, and had reported him to the Security Police. Another student, a girl who was with the first one, caught up with the teacher a block from his apartment building and warned him before he walked into the range of the waiting Sepos. He had been on the run for five days. Twice he had nearly been caught. Suddenly his teeth began to chatter again; then the rigor passed.

He was a lunatic, Rankin thought. A poor, pathetic lunatic.

But they would not view it that way. They would kill him.

The teacher still sat huddled on the edge of the pier. "You think I'm crazy. I'm not. "

Rankin felt the fear squeezing his insides. When he spoke, the words seemed to hang like a cartoon balloon in the air between them.

"Get out of here. Now!"

The man did not move. Rankin jerked him up by his arm. It felt through the torn, shabby jacket like a stick that might snap. Rankin propelled him toward the fence.

"Climb, " he snarled.

The teacher sagged against the fence. "I can't. "

Rankin stared at the pale, sweating face, then toward the street.

"You will. You got in, now get out, damn you!"

The teacher hooked his fingers between the links and began to climb but, after a couple of feet, slid back down. Rankin felt sweat begin to bead his own forehead. He looked toward the street again, then back at the teacher, and felt hate for the man. He knelt down and told the teacher to climb on his shoulders. When he straightened up, he was barely conscious of the other's weight.

"Stand up. You ought to be able to grab the top of the fence. "

He felt the other teetering on his shoulders.

"See that light over there. " It was less than a quarter-of-a-mile away. "That's a marine supply store. They've got a boat there. Now haul yourself over!"

"I don't think I can make it. "

Rankin began to boost him, a hand under each worn shoe

sole. At the same instant he heard a squeal of brakes near the gate; then he was squinting into a bright glare of light.

They were like two flies, he thought, trapped against a chain-link web. Then the teacher fell, landing awkwardly on his side next to Rankin. He groaned and staggered to his feet, clutching his ribs.

From the car a loudspeaker ordered them not to move. Doors slammed and figures appeared at the gate, two helmeted men and a woman, bent and spindly, who pointed in their direction excitedly. Rankin's body felt numb but his mind, with a strange kind of detachment as though he were outside of himself, pieced everything together in a second. The woman must have followed the teacher, seen him and Rankin together and informed. Now both of them were dead men. She would have the reward, and they would be in the morgue. The way his mind seemed to quietly accept these facts told Rankin he must be in some kind of shock.

The teacher was whispering something to him, his lips barely moving.

"Your only chance is the river. You'll have a couple of seconds. Get ready. "

Rankin's feet seemed rooted to the ground as though he were in a trance. He watched the teacher slowly raise his hands and start to advance toward the gate and, out of the tail of his eye, glimpsed the dark water a few yards away. His muscles tensed, and for a moment, he could barely breathe. The beam from the spotlight was blotted out by the teacher's body that was now directly between Rankin and the two Sepos at the gate.

"Now, " hissed the teacher.

One of the Sepos shouted something; the teacher stumbled as the laser beam shot through his body and beyond Rankin, who whirled toward the water and reached it in a flat dive, its cold stunning him like a blow. Then he was beneath the surface, kicking frantically away from the bank. He swam until his lungs were ready to explode.

When he surfaced, he was well below the two men racing toward the bank who were outlined by the spotlight's beam that also revealed the motionless body face down near the water. Rankin had gone under again, felt the fierce pull of the current, and had let it carry him.

He hurried down the street past the boarded-up windows. On the other side was another alleyway, and he started toward it. Half-way across he heard the rumble of an engine. He made it into the alley just as the truck rounded the corner of a side street and its headlight beams almost caught him. He flattened against a slimy brick wall, the acrid smell of urine in his nostrils, as the truck rolled past; then he heard it brake. A voice shouted; there was the clank of a tailgate dropping; boots thudded against pavement; weapons clattered. Rankin risked a quick glance and saw the troopers begin to fan out, up and down the street. He turned and bolted as fast as he could down the alley. With his bad leg he knew he could not outrun them long.

Panting harshly, he reached the next street, ran blindly down it until he came to an overgrown, vacant lot. He dropped into the tall, wet weeds and smelled the damp earth and heard footsteps coming from the direction of the alley. The footsteps drew closer until they were almost abreast of him, then stopped. Rankin almost stopped breathing and kept his head down. His face was pressed against the moist ground but, out of the corner of his eye, he saw the spurt of sudden flame, the tip of a cigarette begin to glow, and the helmeted face of a black man. He shook the match and the flame went out. Another soldier was with him.

"Come on. You got it lit now," the other soldier said impatiently.

"You think he got this far from the river?" The black man's voice was soft.

"Who knows?"

"I wonder what he did?"

"Does it make any difference?"

They started moving away.

"Maybe we'll get lucky and nail him, whoever he is."

"If it limps shoot it, Sarge said."

"Yeah."

Rankin waited several minutes before he dared take a full breath. His eyes stung. Despite the coolness of the night, they were filled with sweat. The soldiers' voices still seemed to echo in his ears. I wonder what he did? What he had done was to be stupid. He had broken the cardinal rule; never be caught helping an enemy of the state.

In trying to help the teacher, he had become an enemy of the state himself.

CHAPTER THREE

The streets were deserted. For all intents he could have been in a ghost city. Although it was not yet midnight, no traffic moved and no pedestrians were abroad but himself. He kept to the shadows and alleys whenever possible. Except for the widely-spaced street lights and a few scattered lights burning in the windows of apartments he passed, the city was nearly as black as it had been for air raids during the war. No electric signs blazed over shops and businesses, restaurants or nightclubs. Since the war, electricity, like food, was severely rationed—coal, petroleum, and plutonium that fueled the power plants were being stockpiled, it was rumored, for the next war. If the winter was severe, some people froze in their homes from lack of heat.

Rankin headed east in the opposite direction from the river. His first impulse had been to go by his one-room apartment and get a few of his belongings. But they would probably already have his identity and be there waiting in case he showed up.

He had little of value in the apartment anyway—some cheap clothes, a few approved books, mostly adventure novels and travel books, a purple heart and a good conduct medal from the war, a few tins of food, and the one thing he really cared about: the framed photograph of Peg and Suzie taken just before he had been air-lifted to England. He realized with a pang he would never see the photograph again. And the Sepos would grab the tins of food, if the apartment manager did not beat them to it. But, right now, the photograph seemed infinitely more valuable to him than food.

He emerged from a narrow side street onto a big open area

stretching for nearly a block. There were a lot of such open areas in the city—places where bombs had fallen. The rubble had been cleared away but, in the seven years since the war there had been little re-building. He stared across the open space uneasily. When he had first come back from the war, such places had made him feel like he was in a strange city—familiar landmarks he had once known had disappeared with only hugh craters or piles of brick and jagged stone to mark where they had been. Now, the space in front of him represented danger. He could skirt it, of course, but it would take more time, and he was anxious to put as much distance between himself and the riverfront as quickly as possible.

He decided to chance it and cut directly across. He had taken only two steps when the black cruiser appeared around the corner a block away. He leaped back into a doorway and flattened himself against the cold stone. The cruiser glided by like an ominous spider.

Rankin barely breathed until the slight hum of its engine had completely faded. Then he darted across the empty space. Halfway across, a sheet of newspaper blew in front of him, momentarily causing his heart to skip. He felt like a thousand pairs of eyes were watching him from the darkened windows in the tall buildings ringing the cleared ground. And, he dreaded the appearance of another cruiser. When he reached the other side and another small side street, he was drenched in sweat.

He was in a neighborhood of rickety wooden houses. He had come a long way from the river and his legs ached. He needed to find some place to hide before dawn. The chances were his face would be on wallscreens during the morning news. His few acquaintances, he had no close friends, no doubt would be shocked over their cups of coffee. One or two that he called friends would also be sympathetic, but terrified that he might contact them for help. He would not. From now on he could afford no friends, nor could they afford him. As he passed some garbage cans, he stumbled and almost fell over a pair of legs protruding onto the sidewalk. One of the legs twitched and a groan came from behind the cans. The man reeked of cheap gin. His bullet-shaped head moved slightly, then settled back onto the concrete. In a moment he was lost again in alcoholic dreams. Rankin hurried on, driven by one thought—the need to find a hideout. Gradually, a plan formed in his mind as he left the poorer section and entered an area of drab concrete apartment buildings five or six stories high. He had worked on one of them before the war. They were constructed cheaply—unadorned cubes designed to pack a lot of people in a minimum amount of space.

He moved swiftly through a pool of light from a streetlamp. Far away he heard the sound of a truck motor, but it died away. As he neared the first apartment building, he cut down an alley between two dingy shops. At the end of the alley he came out onto a parking area; he crossed it and approached the apartment building from the rear. No lights were on in any of the windows, but the front entrance had been lit and certainly locked. So was the rear entrance. He edged along the side of the building and found what he was searching for behind some scrawny shrubbery.

With his pocket knife he pried off the louvered cover to an air vent. He could barely squeeze through the opening, and he dropped down into the basement. In the darkness he was surrounded by the hum of machinery. A light bulb glowed dimly at the top of a flight of stairs. He mounted the stairs, opened the door beneath the light, and found himself in the fire exit stairwell. He cracked a door opposite him and glimpsed a small foyer, an elevator, and a narrow corridor with apartment doors on either side. He shut the door and walked up to the second floor, opened another door, and stole out into the corridor. On the doors of the apartments lining the corridor were name cards, and he read each intently. All had a "Mr. " or "Mr. " and "Mrs., " except one near the end of the hallway. The card read "Miss Lucinda Burke, " and the number on the door was 27. He wondered how old she was, if she had children in there or a live-in boyfriend. Most of all he wondered if she owned a car. Behind him he heard the elevator rising in the shaft. He ran back down the hallway and into the stairwell. The elevator continued to rise and stopped on one of the upper floors. He considered going back to 27 and attempting to break in now, but decided it was too risky. If the woman were to awake and scream, it would bring the whole building down on him.

He started up the stairs, determined to check the other floors. On the sixth floor he finally came across one other single woman's prefix on the door, but it was not as convenient as 27. If he had to escape in a hurry, a drop from the sixth floor would be fatal, while a drop from a second story window, unless he landed very badly, might offer no more than a sprained ankle.

Miss Burke in number 27 it would have to be, he thought.

If he were lucky, she would be going to work in the morning, and he could break in while she was gone. If not, he would have to gain entry under some pretext. He walked slowly down again to the second floor. His leg muscles felt weak, his legs rubbery. The hard swim, the long walk from the river, and the tension all combined to make him feel wearier than he had ever felt in his life, even in combat. He felt with each step as though he were going to collapse. He wanted to sleep, his body craved it fiercely, as did his brain.

When he reached the second floor, he forced himself to go back to the door of 27 and listen intently. There was no sound. It was still far too early for anyone to be stirring except a hard-core insomniac. For a moment, he wanted to break in now and take his chances while whoever was in there was still deep in sleep. But he resisted the impulse. It would be safer to wait until morning and find out if the woman really lived alone. At the opposite end of the corridor from the stairwell was a door he guessed to be a utility room. He had noticed one on each floor and now he walked over to the door and turned the knob. It was unlocked.

The small space contained a fuse box and three trash cans—all almost empty. He closed the door and hunkered down between the cans in the pitch blackness and waited for morning.

The eyes, deep in the hollow sockets, pleaded for help. The gaunt face of the teacher was almost skull-like. His mouth moved and words came out, but Rankin could not make out what he said. Suddenly the teacher was lying face down in the mud, and his back was scorched and smoking.

Rankin groaned and jerked his head up. His forehead was moist with sweat and his throat was sore. He had been asleep. For a moment he had no idea where he was. He was in pitch darkness and his legs had fallen asleep. He reached out and felt the smooth plastic curve of a trash can. Then he remembered.

He heard a voice in the corridor and the sound of the elevator door closing. What time was it? He scrambled to his feet and almost fell because of the numbness in his legs. Bracing himself against the door, he waited until the blood started flowing in them again and a thousand little needles pricked his calves. Quietly he opened the door an inch. No one was in the hallway. He stared at the door of number 27. He held his watch up to the crack. Despite his swim, it was still working, at least the second hand was still moving. It was almost 7:30.

During the next half hour several people left their apartments—but the door to 27 remained shut. Perhaps she was the one he had heard going down in the elevator when he awoke. He dared not risk going out into the hallway right now, while people were still leaving for work. He would have to stay where he was a while longer, and hope nobody would come to empty trash. If they did, he would flick on the light and pretend to be checking the fuse box.

After half an hour the door to 27 swung open and a woman stepped out into the hallway. She was small and slender. She looked to be in her late twenties. Dressed in a gray pantsuit, purse slung under her arm, she walked to the elevator, and he got a good look at her face. She was pretty in a doll-like, vapid sort of way. As she waited for the elevator, the door whooshed shut, and the machinery rattled her down to the first floor.

Quickly, before he could lose his nerve, he darted down the hallway to her door. He slid the blade of his knife between the lock and jamb and waited for the click. All the locks in these buildings were cheap. He cast a quick glance up and down the hall.

He felt the lock give.

He twisted the door knob and let himself into the apartment.

He found himself in a neat, sparsely furnished room that held a modern sofa, a pair of end tables, two orange straight-backed chairs, a low coffee table, and a small wallscreen about three feet in diameter. At the far end of the room was the kitchenette area.

He shut the door behind him and locked it. He sprang across the thin carpet to the window that looked out over the parking lot, in time to see the woman getting into a little silver two-seater. So she had an automobile! He watched her drive out of the lot.

Turning back to the apartment, he discovered a bedroom and small bath. A lot of space for one person, he thought. He lived in one room barely the size of her bedroom. She must know somebody, since apartments of comparable size usually were reserved for couples, many of them with children.

Perhaps she was married, but her husband was working in another city. He checked the bedroom closet and her bureau and found only women's clothing. Back in the living room, he turned on the wallscreen, careful to keep the volume low so no one in adjoining apartments could hear. He checked all the local channels, but the morning news was over and nothing of interest was on. He switched it off and went into the kitchenette area. There was a microwave and a wallfridge. He opened the latter and took inventory—juices, soya concentrate, frozen veggies, nutrabars, and a couple of bottles of California Burgundy. He took a nutrabar, wolfed it down, then went back to the wallscreen and went through the channels again. Still nothing. He began to study the room in a more leisurely fashion.

The furniture was functional but, except for the orange chairs, severe, lacking in warmth. There were no books and only two or three magazines—two of them fashion quarterlies. The other, on closer scrutiny, was not a magazine, but a technical manual on the I-5000 Digital Computer. If she worked with computers, she was probably with the government, which would explain the automobile and apartment. Some single working women might be able to afford a car, but not the fancy little number she had gotten into a few minutes before. Most cars you saw were of pre-war vintage. Of course, there was the possibility she had a rich lover. The walls were basic hospital white, he noticed, continuing his inspection. There was only one picture—an abstract painting in blues and greens that suggested an underwater scene.

The woman's eyes, as she had looked in his direction, were almost the same color as the painting and had given him the impression of cool distance.

He decided that, despite its relative spaciousness, he did not really care for the apartment. No matter. He would not be staying here that long. He had to escape the city and she, with her fancy car, was going to help him. Undoubtedly, she would not like it. He could not blame her. But he would use force if he had to—maybe he would not have to—he hoped he would not.

His gaze flicked to the wallscreen. The face of the school teacher stared back.

"Samuel Ross, an enemy of the state, who had been at large for the past week, was killed last night by Security Police," intoned the newscaster. "So may perish all enemies of the state. He was killed while trying to make his escape by way of the river, authorities say, but not before he attempted to blow up a barge depot. Luckily he was discovered before he could carry out his insidious plan. Mrs. Annie Mae Gilcrest received the reward for spotting him and leading the authorities to the depot. Congratulations, Mrs. Gilcrest!"

Rankin gazed at the black and white face of the school teacher and remembered the man's eyes in the flashlight beam, filled with fear yet also defiance.

Ross had saved his life. The school teacher knew he did not have much longer to live; yet even a few hours, a few minutes were precious, and he had given them up to save Rankin.

Rankin felt his throat tighten.

Then Ross's face vanished and was replaced with his own. He recognized the photograph as the one from his employee file taken three-and-a-half years ago.

"This man is Thomas Rankin, age 32, " said the screen. "He was detected trying to help Samuel Ross escape. He jumped into the river, but is believed to still be alive and hiding somewhere in the city. He has been declared an enemy of the state. Let me repeat—this man, Thomas Rankin, is an enemy of the state. The authorities have posted the usual reward for his death and one half the reward for information leading directly to his capture. Ross was aided by Rankin in his attempt to blow up the depot. Rankin is six feet tall and walks with a limp. He is to be regarded as extremely dangerous . . . . "

Rankin flipped off the switch and watched his face abruptly collapse in on itself, then disappear. If only he could disappear like that—be the disappearing man. He felt like he had been hit in the stomach.

Until now, he realized, a part of him had held on to the slim hope, no matter how absurd, that what had happened last night was not irrevocable. He slumped down on the sofa, his mind awhirl and stared at the blank wallscreen. Finally, he got up, went to the fridge, got one of the wine bottles out, and uncorked it.

He took a couple of long pulls.

Afterward, he went into the bedroom and lay on the bed. He felt immensely tired but could not sleep. He would have to be the disappearing man or he would be a dead man. From now on those were his only choices. He got up and went into the bathroom and took a warm shower. When he got out, he lay again on the strange bed and stared at the ceiling. After a while, he felt himself begin to drift toward sleep.

He dreamed an old woman in a black shawl was pursuing him wherever he went. He ducked into basements, clambered over junkyards, but she was always close behind him and gaining. He sobbed and swore, but he could not shake her. Then he came to a crowded street.

"He's mine!" she screamed and everyone turned to stare at him. Their faces were blank and empty, but the old woman's was contorted with madness. "He's mine!"

He awoke in cold terror.

Around the city, perhaps thousands of people prayed they would be lucky enough to find him. If given the chance, some would only inform on him because they lacked the strength or weapons to kill him or had a squeamish streak. Others, driven by hunger or greed, would kill him instantly if the opportunity came. Still others would do it for the thrill—like killing a large and maybe dangerous animal. And, it would be perfectly legal according to the July Decrees that had been upheld by the Supreme Court.

The military had passed the Decrees while he was in England, right after they had taken over the government. American cities had been bombed. Both sides had agreed in advance not to use nuclear warheads for fear of radioactive contamination of the entire planet. But conventional bombs had virtually leveled New York and Los Angeles, Detroit and Chicago; people were outraged and frightened and turned against the civilian government. So, the generals took over—not without some protest but, with more cities being bombed every day and the threat of invasion from Siberia, they had pulled a lightning coup. The July Decrees were passed—anyone who opposed the new government was a subversive—guilty of treason and, therefore, an "enemy of the state. " It was not only the right, but the duty of all loyal citizens to destroy such enemies. The government would officially declare who these enemies were and, after that, it was open season on them. Of course, there had been critics of this policy, but it had been argued that during a national emergency such as the nation had never faced before, the drastic step was necessary. When the war was over, the Decrees would be revoked and the civilian government would be again reestablished.

The war lasted two years—both sides were devastated and, even though Western Europe was overrun, it was clear that neither side could decisively knock the other out in a conventional war. And, neither side dared resort to nuclear war. So, they had declared a truce—an uneasy one that was still in existence after seven years, but neither side trusted the other. Each believed that the other was only waiting for a favorable opportunity to attack with a newly developed ultimate weapon each was supposedly working on night and day—the space laser. So, both sides awaited the next round, and the military in Washington had not stepped down. They had declared that although the bombing and actual fighting had stopped, the nation just be kept in a state of readiness only they could insure.

At the time, there had been a storm of protest. Factory workers had struck and college students had rioted. People were shot by troops, others shipped off to concentration camps and not heard from again. The military took over the large farms and controlled food distribution. They continued rationing in peace time as one way to control the people. And, they kept the July Decrees as another. The July Decrees had become an instrument of state policy. The size of rewards had been increased.

With nearly a third of the work force unemployed because of robots and automation, the enemy-of-the-state policy was looked upon by many as a kind of lottery or unexpected windfall for anyone lucky enough to chance across a Samuel Ross—or now himself. Rankin rubbed his temples with his knuckles. And, of course, along with the reward would go the knowledge that one was fulfilling his patriotic duty. The result was that thousands of people had become bounty hunters, killing for cash. The Supreme Court had declared it perfectly legal.

Yet, murder was still punishable by a stiff jail sentence. The state defined what killings were murder, as always.

Rankin got off the bed and smoothed out the wrinkles on the spread. He looked out the window at the parking lot.

Two small boys were playing marbles. They had chalked in a circle and now squatted around it intently as one of them prepared to shoot. Across the lot a young woman wheeled a baby buggy. She stopped, leaned over the buggy and re-arranged a pink blanket. She straightened up and, for a moment, she seemed to be looking directly at him. He ducked back behind the drapes, his heart suddenly pounding. Half a minute passed before he dared peer out from the corner of the window. The woman was gone. He scanned the parking lot, then saw her almost beneath him, wheeling the buggy past the two marble players in leisurely fashion, her face placid. If she had seen him, she evidently had not recognized him, he told himself, but it was fifteen minutes before he felt reasonably calm again.

He had to get out of the city soon. Two boys playing marbles, a young mother with a baby were his enemies now. In the city, eyes were everywhere, in parking lots, in other windows, in passing cars, on the streets—you could never hide from them all. It would only be a matter of time before somebody spotted you, as the old woman had spotted Ross. In the country there would be fewer eyes, fewer potential killers. He felt almost like leaving for there right now.

He had to get a grip on himself. He went and got a drink of water from the tap in the little sink. Then he began to pace the apartment and wondered when the woman would return.

The late afternoon sun cast long shadows across the parking lot. Cars had begun to fill it up again, one was parked over the chalked circle where the marble game had been played, as people returned from work. From the corner of the window Rankin watched a tired-looking middle-aged man in a corporate uniform emerge from a small maroon runabout and walk toward the building's rear entrance. He was followed by another man carrying a slim-line briefcase, who was in turn followed by a trim woman in another corporate uniform who was in her middle thirties. They were like puppets moving in a straight line, looking neither right nor left, up or down, simply intent on getting into the building and into their small apartments and probably into a big drink.

Across the lot Rankin noticed an urchin dressed in rags. He leaned against the wire mesh fence that separated him from the lot and stared at the shiny cars parked there. He could not have been more than nine or ten years old, but he eyed the cars greedily. At last he walked away. Several yards from the fence he stooped and picked up a small stone. He hurled it over the fence. It struck the gull-wing door of a black and gold Ramfire, the fastest and newest car in the lot. The boy raced away down the street, his dirty-blond hair flying.

Rankin smiled. He knew how the boy felt.

He wanted to throw something, do anything—his muscles were tight and his nerves strained. The waiting was getting to him. For a moment he wanted to run like the boy, run with him, match him stride for stride, outstrip him, race beyond the reach of the Sepos and their scorching lasers. He turned away from the reflection of his own face in the glass and gazed for the hundredth time around the sterile apartment. He felt as though he would jump out of his skin.

As he turned back to the window, the silver two-seater pulled into the lot. The woman parked it in a slot between two larger cars. She got out and the sun glinted on her dark hair. Like the others, she marched toward the rear entrance without a glance upward or to her left or right. He was relieved that she was alone. If she had brought a friend, he would have had to get out and abandon the plan and run the grave risk of being seen in the hallway or on the stairwell.

He walked swiftly into the bedroom and, like a bad joke in an old movie, crawled under the bed.

The seconds dragged by. At last he heard the hallway door close behind her, the lock snap, then brisk footsteps as she walked into the living room, paused, then came into the bedroom. She paused again. The mattress sagged down on him as she sat on the bed. Her ankles covered by the gray pant suit were inches from his hand. She kicked off one shoe and pulled off the other. She stood up. The gray pants snaked to the floor, followed by white panties. He smelled her fragrance. The pants and panties were scooped up, her bare ankles retreated into the bathroom. The bathroom door closed and, in a minute, the shower came on. He wriggled out from under the bed, got to his feet, and stood awkwardly by the bureau. He had violated her apartment, but he could not bring himself to intrude upon her in her bath and wondered at his own weird sense of propriety. Just by his presence he was endangering her life; yet, while she remained in the shower, she seemed too vulnerable. Let her have a few minutes more of privacy before he changed the current of her life, just as Ross had changed his.

When the water shut off, he stood beside the bathroom door, his back pressed against the wall.

She came out, draped in a thick towel and steam around her. She did not even see him as she passed.

He clamped a hand over her mouth, his other arm shot around her waist and pulled her against him.

"Listen to me carefully." he whispered. "Don't shout or scream and I won't hurt you. You understand?"

Her muscles were so taut they almost vibrated.

"Understand?"

She nodded. Her flesh was still warmly moist from the shower, her hair damp. She smelled strongly of perfumed soap.

"I'm not here to rob you or to molest you. But right now I don't have anywhere else to go, so I'm going to have to stay here for a short while. Now I'm going to take my hand away. But if you scream, I'll tie you up and gag you. "

Her shoulder muscles quivered against him.

Slowly he took his hand away. Then he released her. She turned, her face pale and taut. Her eyes widened and he saw the flicker of recognition in them.

"You know who I am. And you know I don't have anything left to lose. So don't do anything stupid. "

"What do you want?" Her voice was low, but did not quaver. Without makeup her face looked ghostly.

"Food and shelter until early morning. Then I'll be gone. "

She clutched the towel more tightly around her small breasts. She stared at him, but there seemed no emotion in those still blue-green eyes, not even fear. Again he was reminded of the abstract painting on the wall in the other room—like the painting, there was a cool, depthless quality in her gaze.

"Well. " Her eyes never wavered from his. "Are you going to let me get dressed?" A drop of water traced a wet ribbon down her thigh.

He nodded, his eyes on the drop.

She turned her back on him and walked into the closet. She did not bother to close the door behind her. She padded back with clothes on her arm and laid them on the bed. She went to the bureau and got underthings out of a drawer.

"Could I get dressed without an audience?"

"Go back into the closet. "

He would not leave her alone in the bedroom and give her a chance to signal out the window, or even perhaps jump. It was only a fifteen-foot drop. She whipped the clothes off the bed and went into the closet. This time, she pulled the door shut behind her.

She did not take long. She came out in a white silk blouse and black stretch pants. Without a glance at him, she went to the mirror above the dresser and began brushing her dark hair in swift, hard strokes.

He watched her watching her own reflection in the glass.

"Why me?" she said at last, still looking at herself, and not him. There was no emotion in her voice. "Of all the apartments and all the people in the city, why me?"

CHAPTER FOUR

When he did not reply, she turned from the mirror and looked at him, the hairbrush clutched tightly in her hand. Outside, a car started up in the parking lot. Through a crack in the drawn drapes twilight filtered into the room. Very carefully, she set the brush down on the dresser, then walked into the other room. He followed her.

She went to a cabinet above the refrigerator and pulled out a bottle of Scotch. She reached into another cabinet and got a glass. She poured three fingers of Scotch into the glass and drank half of it in a gulp. Then the rest of it in another gulp and without a shudder.

"I wouldn't mind a little of that, " he said.

She shrugged, pulled out another glass, and gestured for him to pour his own. He did, while she opened the refrigerator and brought out some vegetables and soya concentrate. She got out a sauce pan from another cabinet and poured the concentrate in and added some water. Her movements were brusque, and she kept her back to him. He poured a couple of fingers of Scotch into his glass and walked over to the wallscreen and switched it on. He sipped the Scotch. It was good. He had not drunk Scotch in years, could not afford it.

He switched over the channels looking for the news. On the Hong Kong channel, a Filipino rock group called "Mooning the Drill Team" mouthed obscenities to a catchy beat. On another, a middle-aged woman with the air of a professor discussed the benefits of laser massage for breast development. Another was showing an old war movie, another a commercial for abortion candy. He turned it off.

"I guess it's too early for the news. " He finished his Scotch and felt the warm glow spread in his belly. She had put the veggies in another pan and put both of them in the microwave. She had a small kitchen knife in her hand.

She turned to him. "Why are they after you. "

He eyed the knife. A fragment of carrot peel still clung to its sharp edge.

"You recognized me. You must have seen what they said. "

She placed the knife in the sink and poured herself another drink from the bottle. She stared at him over the rim of the up-tilted glass. He wondered if she always drank like this or if it was simply from fear. Except for the first few moments when he had grabbed her, she had displayed little fear. It was as if there was a certain deadness inside her, but that could be an effect of shock or dread at his sudden materialization in her home, in her bedroom. To her, he must be a nightmare in the flesh.

She lowered the glass and licked a drop of whiskey from her lower lip. Her pale face without make-up added to the impression of deadness.

"They say you are an enemy of the state. And that is what I'll be if they catch you here. "

She finished her drink.

"Is that what you want? To bring me down with you? "

"No. I don't want that. "

"Then why don't you just leave. It's almost dark. In another few minutes you can slip out of the building and nobody will be the wiser. I won't tell on you. "

"Sure, you wouldn't. "

"I wouldn't. Just go. Do you think I would want to implicate myself? I don't want to get involved. They might even say I tried to shelter you and only got cold feet after you left. "

"I'm hungry, " he said.

"Yes. You can eat. Then will you go?"

"Your hospitality is overwhelming. "

Her face went a little whiter, but she turned to the microwave.

In a few minutes she handed him a plate of food and a cup of ersatz coffee. The food was not too palatable to begin with, but clearly cooking was not one of her talents. Still, he needed the nourishment, and he wolfed the food down while she picked at a smaller portion in her own plate.

"What do you do?" he said.

She gave up the pretense of eating and put her plate down on the counter.

"Computers, " she said tonelessly. "I'm a technician. "

He put his plate down. This was one of the most miserable meals he had ever eaten and, undoubtedly, it was for her too. He felt a stab of pity for her. But he needed her and, if he had little chance of escaping the city with her, he thought he had even less of a chance without her.

"How did you get this?" He indicated the apartment with a sweep of his hand.

"My ex-husband. " She folded a paper napkin and unfolded it. "He works in city housing. "

"Any children?" He had not seen any pictures. A mother would have pictures, he told himself.

"That's none of your business, " she said.

"You're right. It's not. You've got wine in your refrigerator. Would you like some?"

"No. But help yourself by all means. "

She began to clean the plates in the sink. Suddenly she whirled around.

"Look. I want to know what you plan to do with me. "

He sipped the wine he had just poured.

"I plan to blow up the whole apartment building. I'm a dangerous saboteur. "

The blue-green eyes fixed him icily. Behind them, for the first time, he detected a dangerous glitter, but her face remained a pale mask.

"I want to know, " she repeated.

He put down the wine glass. He would have to tell her sooner or later, so why not now. He started to speak and the telephone rang. They both jerked their heads toward it. It rang again, and she stood poised as if to answer it then looked at him.

"Let it ring. "

"It's a friend. He promised to call. If I don't answer, he'll worry. "

"Let him worry. "

"I told him I would be in. He might come over. "

"All right. Answer it and get rid of him. " He grabbed her wrist tightly. "And be very careful. "

He picked up the receiver and handed it to her, at the same time increasing the pressure on her wrist. She glared at him defiantly, and he relaxed the pressure a bit, but gave her a warning look.

"Hello, " she said into the receiver.

He put his head close to the receiver. A man's voice spoke on the other end, but it was a muffled garble to Rankin, and he pressed his face closer until his cheek almost touched hers.

"I'm sorry, Frank, " she said. "I can't tonight. "

Rankin nodded at her.

"No. I'm tired, Frank. Really I am. "

The voice on the other end became slightly querulous.

"No, not even a nightcap. I think I'm coming down with . . . a headache. " Her voice quavered between a sob and a laugh.

Rankin squeezed her wrist.

"Tomorrow, " she said. "Call me tomorrow, will you?"

Rankin motioned for her to cut it off. The voice on the other end sounded softer.

"Please, honey. " Her voice became softer too. "I feel the same way. " She turned from Rankin. "Me too. Bye. "

Rankin hung up the receiver. Releasing her wrist, he walked over and flicked on the wallscreen. She picked up his wine glass from the counter and drained the rest of the drink. Her hand trembled on the stem. She smashed the glass against the wall; shards sailed around her. The tiny slivers shone on the floor. A few were at his feet, flittering like mica.

No news was on the wallscreen.

"Why don't you leave?" she whispered. "Get out of the city. "

"I will—in the morning. I'm going to need your car. "

She gave a short laugh.

"And I'll need you too. "

She stared at him. "You're crazy! "

"We'll be a nice married couple. "

"No! They'll recognize you at one of the checkpoints. They'll think I'm helping you!"

"I need your identity card, which means I need you to get through the checkpoint. You'll be driving. They'll check your card. "

"Even if they don't recognize you, they will check yours too. "

He shook his head. "Maybe not. We'll go through at rush hour. Plus, I'll be sick, and you'll be rushing me to the hospital— St. Francis—which is a couple miles outside the city. The guards will have their hands full checking just the drivers' I.D. 's. I don't think they'll want to bother with a sick passenger.

"They'll still recognize your face. "

"Maybe. But they won't expect me to be with a woman. And I'll use your make-up brush to do a little work on my face. A small mustache for one thing. "

"It will never work. "

She was probably right. But there was a chance that it might. And, better to take that chance than to run around the city in circles like Ross until they harried you like a cat with a mouse to your doom. A big plastics factory lay across from the hospital. If they could get into the traffic flow for the morning shift between 7:00 and 8:00 going to the factory, they might slip through just possibly.

"I won't do it. "

"You will if I have to strap you behind the wheel and tie your foot to the accelerator. I told you I have nothing to lose. "

"But I do, damnit!" Her eyes were like the splintered shards from the wine glass. "You'll get me killed. It's not fair. "

Suddenly he felt very tired.

His picture came on the wallscreen. It was the same one they had used earlier, and the same spiel, with only two additions. The first was that he and Ross were thought to be enemy agents, which accounted for them trying to blow up the barge depot. The second was that, while Rankin was still thought to be at large in the city, the security police expected to apprehend him very soon.

The woman gazed at his picture on the screen, as though looking at a freak in a carnival.

Rankin's picture was replaced by a beautiful woman with gleaming teeth selling dental floss.

Lucinda Burke's gaze drifted to the fragments of glass on the floor at her feet.

"Do you believe that tripe?" Rankin asked. "Do you really believe I would try to blow up a place where I worked for nearly four years. "

She walked past him toward the counter and her foot crunched on a piece of glass. She got another wine glass from the cabinet and poured wine into it. She swirled the contents of the glass, as though she could read something in its ruby flickerings.

He crunched over the broken glass to her and leaned close.

"I saw a man killed last night because he nailed up some pieces of paper. He didn't try to blow up anything. He was sick and alone and scared. I tried to help him get into a boat and just drift down river. I was scared. I didn't want him around, but I didn't want him to die either for such a—a little thing. Now, they are trying to kill me. I don't like dragging you into this, believe me. "

"But you are, aren't you. " She took a long drink of the wine. She picked up the bottle and walked over to the uncomfortable-looking sofa and sat down. She stared abstractedly at the wallscreen, where a man with a pet penguin trudged through Antarctic snow. The penguin, wings at its side, waddled after the man like a Charlie Chaplin drunk.

Luncinda Burke finished the wine in her glass and poured some more from the bottle.

By herself she had finished the wine in the bottle. It was getting late. She had not said anything to Rankin, but only stared at the shifting images on the wallscreen. Once she had gotten up to go to the bathroom, and Rankin had followed her to the bathroom door and made her keep it open. Although there was no window in the room, he thought she might lock herself in and tap on the wall to the next apartment or scream. But she had only relieved herself, then marched back to the couch and resumed her task of finishing off the bottle. For his part, Rankin had been going over and over his escape plan, only too aware of its flaws, but unable to think up an alternative that might improve his changes. He had to get out of the city, and a car and the woman offered the best chance.

She yawned. "I suppose I can go to bed, can't I?" She tried to sound casual, but beneath the soft slurry edge of drink, there seemed another quality, not anxiety, but a kind of, he wanted to say, decisiveness, although he was not sure that was the word to describe it.

"Go to sleep, " he said. "Nobody's stopping you. "

She rose from the couch and started for the bedroom.

"What's wrong with the couch?" he said.

"I can't sleep on it. It's too hard. "

Rankin followed her into the bedroom. She turned and looked him straight in the eyes. "What are you doing? "

"Do you honestly think I can leave you alone in here?"

She shrugged. A shadow flickered behind her eyes. She went into the closet and began to take off her clothes. She did not close the door.

Rankin saw a gleaming bare thigh. He limped to the window,

peered through the crack in the drapes. Below, the parking lot was dark and silent, the street beyond, deserted. He thought again of the urchin running down it, ragged but free. Or, at least with the illusion of freedom. He turned and Lucinda Burke was wearing a black negligee. Rankin stared at her while his throat tightened.

She walked over to the bed and pulled down the cover. As she bent, he saw the dark valley between her small, firm breasts. She straightened and met his gaze. He wanted her and she knew it. She had primed herself for him with enough alcohol to give someone twice her size delirium tremens. He admired her capacity.

Still watching him, she got into bed.

He pulled out the draw cord from the drapes as her eyes widened.

"What's . . . that for?"

He sat down on the bed and grasped her wrist. He slipped the cord around it.

"Don't. "Don't tie me up, " she pleaded. She touched his hand with her free one, her fingers felt warm and silky.

"I need rest—I may fall asleep. I can't take the chance." He wrapped the cord around his own wrist several times. He reached over and flicked out the light then stretched out beside her on his back.

"If you move, I'll know it. "

"What if I have to use the bathroom?"

"Then we'll go together. "

She rolled over on her side, her back to him. He listened to the slow rise and fall of her breathing. After several minutes, she began to fidget. Finally she turned to him.

"I can't sleep this way. "

"Then I guess you're not very sleepy. "

But he could not sleep either. Although he felt exhausted, he was too keyed up, every muscle felt tense, and his calves ached. She lay on her back and, after a while, he thought she must be asleep. Again, he went over his plan for in the morning. She had said he would get her killed. He had to acknowledge that there was a strong possibility she would be. But, without her, he could not run the checkpoint., He could have picked a man, but a man was more dangerous and the Sepos would be more apt to let a woman through, especially if her husband needed an emergency appendectomy, or so he hoped. He tried not to dwell on the idea of her dying, but his mind kept playing the thought over and over.

She turned toward him, startling him out of his thoughts. He waited for her to say something, but she did not and he decided she had shifted her position in her sleep. Again, he felt sympathy for her, one hand bound and a stranger lying next to her only inches away, a stranger who, when dawn came, intended to gamble with her life in an attempt to save his own.

He might wake her up now and try to run the checkpoint in the dark but, with little traffic, they would be more thorough in their examination of identity cards. And, they expected him to try to escape by night, he guessed. That is what he was counting on, that and the fact that he would not have a "wife" according to their records.

The woman stirred; then he felt her body against his. Her free hand moved to his chest, and she began to unbutton his shirt. Her fingertips crept lightly over his bare chest, down his stomach. They began to tug at his belt.

He stared at the dark ceiling. Her fingers found what they sought, and she enclosed him with her mouth. After a while she wriggled over him like a snake and her tongue, tasting of wine, slid slyly into his mouth. He rolled over on her. Her hard little body strained up against him, her hips rose to meet his, the hem of the negligee around her belly.

When they had finished, exhausted and sweating, he rolled off her. They lay still on their backs, their wrists still bound together by the drape cord. All the tension had drained out of him. Her low, steady breathing matched his own. He closed his eyes. His body felt numb, his mind shut off from thought. The steady rhythm of their breathing, like a metronome, lulled him toward sleep. Soon it came on him, but fitfully, like he was going through a series of tunnels instead of one long one. And between tunnels she whispered that she had to use the bathroom, but so low he might have imagined it.

She moved so smoothly and swiftly he did not know she was up, except for the slight rise of the mattress as her weight left it. Dimly it occurred to him that she had removed the cord from her wrist. He heard the toilet flush and tried to remember what he had seen in the bathroom: shampoo, cosmetics, valium — the only things besides those he could think of were a nail file, tweezers, eyelash curler, and a small pair of scissors . . . .

The hair on the back of his neck prickled.

She padded back into the room. She stood a moment by the edge of the bed and, in the darkness, he could barely see her hand rising above her shoulder. He dove off the bed and heard the scissors snick as they plunged into the mattress a split second late.

CHAPTER FIVE

She had flung her body across the bed and, before she could pull the scissors free, he grabbed her wrist and tried to scramble to his feet. But she wrenched away and jerked her arm over her shoulder for another thrust. Her lips lifted from her faintly gleaming teeth as though in a snarl, yet no sound came from her throat. He yanked the pillow from his side of the bed, and when she lunged, the scissors stuck in it instead of him. Before she could stab at him again, he cracked her hard on the side of the jaw. She fell sideways on the bed and dropped the scissors.

He kicked them under the bed, pulled the drape cord free of his own wrist, yanked her arms behind her, and began to tie her up before she could struggle. Suddenly she began to scream. He cut her off in mid-cry with the pillow. She fought but, with her hands tied, she was helpless. Soon she quit thrashing.

"If you scream again, I'll smother you, " he snarled. He tore a strip off the sheet, removed the pillow, and used the strip for a gag. Then he pulled out his pocket knife, cut the drape cord, and tied her feet with part of it.

When he finished, he was panting. He rose from the bed, his flesh clammy, and stared down at her as though she were some alien creature.

My God! She had entwined herself around him in the act of love—then tried to murder him. He began to tremble. And he thought she would not be as dangerous as a man. He felt an urge to laugh and choked it back. He picked up his pants that had been removed while they were making love—he could not remember how or when they had come off, so intent had they been on each other. He struggled into them, then went to the window and looked out. No one was up yet, it was still dark outside. He turned back to her.

"I wasn't going to make you go. " Even though he had not made a conscious decision, he felt it was true. Nor would he force her to drive through the checkpoint now, even though she had tried to murder him.

He rememberd how intently she had watched the wallscreen when his picture had come on, as though she were looking at a freak but, she must have been thinking, a valuable one. She had tried to get him to leave, even then. He supposed that, in a way, he had given her no choice. After he had told her his plan, she must have decided she had no alternative, if she wanted to save her own life. And then there was the reward to spur her on. Finally, to her, it wasn't even murder, but simply her patriotic duty.

He bent over, and she tried to squirm away. He pulled the negligee down that had worked above her hips during their struggle.

Then he left the room, closing the door behind him. He did not really want to look at her again. For a moment he thought he was going to throw up, but the moment passed. The wallscreen still hummed gently. They had not bothered to turn it off when they had left the living room. He turned it off now.

Again he went to the window and peered down at the silver two-seater. In the east, a dull light was beginning to show on the horizon. But, as yet, nobody was out. Now was the time to take the car, before anybody spotted him. Without the woman he had no chance of getting past the checkpoint, but at least he would be better off in the car than on foot. He might find, if he searched hard enough, a road or trail that just possibly was not roadblocked and led out of the city. It was hard to block every exit route. He remembered she had left her purse on the dresser in the bedroom.

Reluctantly, he entered the bedroom again and switched on the light. He emptied the purse's contents on the dresser top and found the car keys. Also, he took the small amount of cash she had in her billfold.

She mumbled something unintelligible through the gag as he pocketed them.

"Bye, darling. Give Frank my regards. " He did not envy Frank.

Her eyes glittered with rage. He turned off the light and closed the door on her. If looks burn like lasers, she would have shrivelled him, he was certain, through the door. He walked swiftly to the refrigerator and took the nutrition bars and stuffed them into his pockets. He hooked the remaining bottle of wine and a pack of matches he found on the counter too.

The corridor was empty when he looked out through the cracked door. He stepped out into the hall, locked the door, shut it behind him, and hurried to the fire stairs.

Outside, in the parking lot the cool, fresh air felt clean and invigorating after his confinement in the apartment with Lucinda Burke. Her car was wet with dew in the semi-darkness. He unlocked the door and got in quickly, inserted the key in the ignition, and switched it on. The engine purred into immediate life. He gazed up through the moist windshield at her bedroom window. Eventually she would work herself free of her bonds or her boyfriend would free her, but by that time he expected he would be dead or out of the city. On the other hand, there was the possibility that someone in the apartment building had seen him from a window get into her car and was dialing the police right now to report a car thief, in which case he would be dead much sooner.

He pushed the gear button and started toward the drive that led to the street. The street was nearly deserted. Only a couple of cars moved on it, their headlights glowed faintly against the gray light of dawn. He fumbled around and found the car's lights and switched them on. He eased the little car out and turned east away from the river and toward Nashville.

The car smelled new. He had not owned one since the war. For many people cars, especially new ones, were no longer affordable. And gas was rationed and expensive. He checked the fuel gauge and, to his dismay, saw the needle rested below empty. He cursed. Why didn't she keep gas in the tank? He had no idea whether he could make it out of the city now, even if he came across a road that was not blocked. There was no way to get gas without a ration book and, if he had one, he would have to show his identity card. Although he was going less than thirty-five, he eased up on the accelerator. He kept glancing at the fuel indicator, hoping the needle was stuck or, that with each passing block, it might somehow read differently.

Within five minutes after he had pulled out of the lot, the motor sputtered and died. He glided over to the curb and tried to start it again, but knew it was futile. Lucinda Burke had had the last laugh.

He looked around him. He was in the middle of a slum ring. He could not have picked a worse place to run out of gas had he tried. Here, the car would attract immediate attention from residents and police alike, since hardly a tenant possessed any kind of automobile except an occasional pre-war clunker. Any minute, he expected a crowd of kids to gather and start prying off the hubcaps. He got out of the car and walked away from it casually, until he turned a corner, then he picked up his pace and began to look for a place to hide. Nobody was in sight on the street, but the eastern sky was flushing pink, and in the crumbling buildings, many people were probably already out of bed. Despite the coolness of the dawn, sweat began to break out on his forehead.

Then, a couple of blocks away, a police car rounded a corner and headed slowly toward him.

His bowels went cold. He stopped and turned into the doorway he was abreast of without thought or hesitation. Confronted by a closed door, he prayed it was not locked. He twisted the knob and the next moment was in in a dank hallway smelling of cabbage and urine. Closing the door behind him, he started for a dim rectangle at the other end, passing several closed doors on either side, and emerged onto a scabby dirt courtyard that led to the rear of an even scabbier-looking tenement.

Crossing the courtyard, he pushed open the rear door and found himself in another foul-smelling hallway and face to face with a rawboned woman with gray straggly hair and a ragged bathrobe.

"What's going on? Who the hell are you?"

"An accident, " he panted. "A woman over there, " he pointed to the building he had just come out of, "Fell down the steps. I'm going after Doc White over on the next block. "

He hurried on, but she followed him.

"I ain't never heard of Doc White. Say, ain't I seen you somewhere? Hey! I know you. " She grabbed Rankin's arm. "You got a limp. You're the one they're lookin' for!" She was shouting.

A door opened ahead of him, and a thin, wiry man stepped into the hallway. He wore only his underwear and smelled of gin, and he held a baseball bat.

"It's him!" screamed the woman. "Charlie, it's the one on TV! The one they're looking for. Get him!"

The man stared at Rankin a moment, and his face split in a lopsided smile. He raised the bat and, still smiling, started for Rankin, but his eyes were hard as stone.

Rankin spun the woman into him, and both toppled back through the doorway from which the man had emerged. The man disengaged himself from her and started back into the hallway. Rankin dropped him with a punch to the belly. He doubled over on his knees and began to gasp for air like someone drowning. The woman gaped goggle-eyed from the man to Rankin and back to the man.

Rankin rushed out the front door into the street before she could bring the inhabitants of the building down on him. Her screams began again. He looked up and down the street. Across it, two kids stared at him from a front stoop. Next to them, a rusty bicycle leaned against the stoop.

Bounding across the narrow street, Rankin snatched up the bike, mounted it, and wobbled away. Behind him came footsteps and he turned to see one of the kids, green snot trickling from his nose, pursuing. He was about ten. "You bastard!" shouted the kid.

Rankin pumped and gradually drew away from him. Ahead the street was a deserted gray expanse of pitted concrete, enclosed on either side with rotting two and three-store tenements. He swung down another narrow street, casting a last glance at the snot-nosed kid who had given up the chase and now stood motionless fifty yards back in baleful silence. Rankin continued to pump furiously. Ahead, he saw an alley and turned into it. For a moment, he had a vision of pedalling all the way out of the city, hunched over the handle bars, bursting through the checkpoint. He had to grin at his own absurdity. The alley took him across two more streets. It was almost as narrow and foul as the hallways he had traversed a couple of minutes earlier. Ahead of him, the alley angled sharply to the left. He started to ease up on the pedals to make the turn when the bike stopped abruptly. The alley and the sky seemed to reverse positions as he cartwheeled over the handlebars.

For an instant, lights exploded behind his eyes. He tried to get up, but a heavy weight settled on his chest. Then he felt something cold and sharp prick against the hollow of his throat.

"Don't move!" a high voice said. For an instant, he thought the snot-nosed kid had somehow caught up with him. But as his vision cleared, the grotesque, mashed features Rankin stared up at were not a child's. The man had powerful shoulders and forearms, but his legs were short and stubby and Rankin realized he was a dwarf. He squatted on Rankin's chest like a gargoyle, and he had a long icepick at Rankin's throat.

The dwarf's eyes were bright—unnaturally bright—and danced with a kind of frenzied excitement. Speed, Rankin guessed. So this is how it was going to end—in a dank alley with the snub nose, undershot jaw and thick lips of a hophead dwarf imprinted forever on his own dead eyeballs.

"You got a bike, " piped the dwarf, "maybe you got money too. "

He's so high he doesn't recognize me, Rankin thought, or else he hasn't seen a TV or wallscreen in the past thirty-odd hours.

He climbed off Rankin's chest, but kept the icepick at a point just beneath his ear. He shoved Rankin on his side, reached and extracted Rankin's wallet from his hip pocket.

Near Rankin's right hand, by a garbage can, lay the bicycle—a broom handle sticking out from the crumpled spokes of the front wheel. The dwarf must have crouched behind the garbage can and stuck the broom handle in the front wheel as Rankin flashed past him. Slowly Rankin's fingers inched toward the smooth handle.

Thumbing through Lucinda Burke's bills in the wallet, the dwarf nodded. Then, he found Rankin's identification card. He screwed up his eyes to read it and suddenly let the icepick slip from its resting place beneath Rankin's ear. His eyes seemed to focus, and he looked at Rankin in wonder.

Rankin seized the broom handle and whipped it across the dwarf's cheek with a stinging crack that toppled him backward. Rankin scrambled to his feet, pain pulsing in his leg where he had scraped it on the pavement.

Fast as a cat, the dwarf regained his feet too, picked up the garbage can lid as a shield, and began to circle Rankin with the icepick poised like a gleaming stiletto.

Rankin feinted with the broom handle, the dwarf danced backward, and Rankin scooped up his wallet from the pavement. It held the only pictures he had left of Peg and Suzie. Above the garbage lid the dwarf's eyes gleamed malevolently. He wore a ratty army field jacket that hung below his knees. He lunged suddenly at Rankin with the icepick, barely missing his groin. In the distance, a police siren wailed. The dwarf cast a quick glance behind him, and Rankin turned and ran.

A few yards ahead the alley ended at an eight-foot high wooden fence. He had to drop the broom handle to scramble over the fence. Behind him he heard footsteps and, as he cleared the top, he glimpsed the snarling face of the dwarf with his yellow, broken teeth, while a gnarled hand thrust the icepick up at him. Then Rankin dropped to the ground on the other side.

The dwarf flung himself against the fence futilely trying to grasp the top and haul himself over. He tried several times.

"Come back," he howled. "You're mine! Mine!"

He began to sob. He plunged the icepick into the fence in frustration, withdrew it, and jabbed it again and again into the fence in a manic fury.

Rankin limped through a weedy vacant lot away from the fence. Now, he was even the quarry for runny-nosed kids and hophead dwarfs. He had to find a hiding place quick. The sun was rising. Its first rays struck the tops of the tenements and gleamed off their upper windows over in the next street.

Behind him, he could hear the dwarf still stabbing at the fence.

"Peg," he whispered. "Peg."

Then he was on the street, similar to the others he had fled down since he abandoned the car, and still empty, but not for much longer. People would be going to work soon, those who had jobs. He passed it, before his mind registered the object. Of course, he should have thought of it before. He gazed up and down the deserted street, took a deep breath, and walked back to the cast-iron manhole cover.

The wail of the police siren drew nearer.

As he slogged and groped his way through the fetid tunnel, he lost all track of time. Now and then he was seized with a claustrophobic panic, and he would stop and light a match to banish the darkness and gain some kind of control of himself. Occasionally he heard slitherings and splashings around him. Once, when he struck a match, he saw an almost impossibly bloated rat directly ahead, staring at him with red eyes. He kicked at it, slipped and nearly fell into the sewage. The rat splashed away like some weird amphibian from a primordial world.

At intervals, he would pass under a manhole where a little light filtered down from a hole or crack. He longed to climb up for a breath of fresh air. He would rest at these places, hearing occasional footsteps and even muffled voices from above, and reflect that he was cut off from that sunlit world of daily errands and exchanged pleasantries by more than a few feet of earth and concrete. At first, he feared he might have been spotted going into the sewer and that he would be pursued. But, as time passed, the fear dwindled, and his hate of the stench and darkness increased. Yet, he knew he would have to stay down here at least until nightfall. He was not sure in which direction he was going, but he thought it was west. Other tunnels intersected with his, but he kept doggedly straight ahead. He felt certain that they would have traced the registration on the abandoned car to Lucinda Burke and released her by now. Having talked to her, the Sepos would seal off every road, path, and rut leading out of the city to the east, north, and south. But, to the west, lay the river. It was not so easily sealed off. They might not expect him to try the river again after what had happened to Sam Ross.

His belly tightened at the thought. But the more he thought about it, the more convinced he became that, right now, the river offered the best chance of escape.

Stuck in this stinking darkness, even death seemed not quite so terrible, if he could feel the fresh river breeze again and see the sky and water.

But, first, he would have to wait until night. How many more hours would that be, he wondered, as he plowed through the flushed turds of three-quarters-of-a-million people.

CHAPTER SIX

Beneath him, at the bottom of the bluff, the river gleamed in the moonlight—a wide, moving road that wound over six hundred miles to the Gulf of Mexico. Rankin watched the lights of a towboat as it nosed a string of barges under the big bridge leading to Arkansas. Because much of the barge cargo was grain, the river was always patrolled. But it would be hard to spot a lone man on the river at night, if he kept along the shadows of the bank. He rose from his hiding place in the weeds and started down the steep bluff toward a Marine Supply Store dock.

Half way down he froze.

Somebody had coughed in the bushes lining the road at the bottom of the embankment. Rankin waited motionless, his eyes fixed on the spot where he had heard it. But he could see nothing except the dark shapes of the bushes.

Where he crouched on the bluff, there was no cover, and the moonlight made him an easy target. Yet he was afraid to move, afraid any movement might attract the attention of somebody below.

He waited what seemed like a long time. Then he heard another cough. They had guessed he might try the river again, and had staked out all the places where he might find a boat. The Marine Supply Store was dark, but a skiff bobbed at the end of the dock. The skiff was the bait they had left for him.

Damn them!

Slowly he began to inch his way back up the bluff. The incline was so steep he had to use his hands to help him climb. He prayed whoever was down there did not look up. Any instant he expected a bullet to slam into him. At last, he reached the crest and crept back into the tall weeds, his heart pounding.

He crept along the top of the bluff, staying in the shadows of the deserted warehouses. It was clear now that he would probably not be able to steal a boat. Nor could he swim very far down the river; he was not that strong a swimmer.

He made his way south in the direction of the bridge, leaving the warehouses behind. If whoever was down there had not coughed, he realized he would probably be dead by now. The thought left him weak. But he was determined now. He would escape by the river tonight or else, like Ross, die in the attempt. There would be no turning back to the city to hide in sewers until he starved or could stand it no longer and came out to be killed by a Sepo or an ordinary citizen or a pack of them. He understood now something of the bleak resignation he had seen in Ross.

Below him lay a dark, empty stretch of bank that covered perhaps a quarter of a mile. His hands began to sweat and his breathing came faster. No docks or boats down there, the bank was too steep and it curved rather sharply. And from the road down to the water was covered by dense underbrush.

He paused a long time, gathering his courage before he began to descend the bluff, crouching low and moving as silently as possible. He reached the road and waited, listening. Then he darted across it into the thick brush, paused and listened again. The only sound was the water lapping against the concrete slabs of the revetment. It took him several minutes to creep through the brush down to the revetment.

Staying close to the water's edge, he rounded the curve and, in the slack water, found among the driftwood and floating debris something that made his heart skip. It was a common enough sight; he had seen hundreds of them washed up on the bank in the past but now, although he had hoped to find one, he had not dared to believe that he would.

With a piece of driftwood, he reached and hauled in the tire.

He crouched beside it and inspected it in the darkness. It ought to keep him afloat; at any rate, he would soon find out. He reached into his pocket and pulled out the last nutribar he had stolen from Lucinda Burke. He would need all his strength. He wished he had the bottle of wine he had taken from her too, but he had abandoned that with the car. The slum kids had probably drunk the wine within minutes after he had gone, while stealing the hubcaps and anything else they could carry away. Maybe they could swap their loot for enough food to forget their hunger for a few hours. He finished the bar.

On the road above, a car drove past slowly. Although it was concealed by the brush, he guessed it was a Sepo cruiser and decided not to wait any longer. Grasping the tire, he waded into the water. In another moment, holding the tire out in front of him, he kicked away from the bank. The water chilled him instantly. Then the current caught him and swept him toward the bridge.

Soon one of its huge piers loomed out of the darkness. It came at him with frightening speed. The fierce current almost tore the tire from his grasp as he struggled to keep from being slammed into the pier. At the last second he swept past it with two feet to spare.

Eighty feet above him stood the dark span, and he heard a voice, probably one of the sentries at the Tennessee checkpoint: " . . . two Texans were taking a leak off this bridge one night and one of 'em says 'Say, the water is cold, ain't it, ' and the other one says, 'Yeah, and it's deep, too.' "

The laughter faded as he drifted past the bridge. In a minute he could see a tiny red glow up there from a cigarette one of the sentries was smoking. It winked brighter, then suddenly arced down toward the water. If they were following it with their eyes, he did not see how they could miss spotting him. But evidently they had better things to do than peer after a discarded cigarette because there was no shout or clamor from the bridge and, within a short time, he was far enough away to breathe more easily again.

Along the bank the few lights gave way to darkness, the dwellings to fields and trees. The current swirled him along and then he was abreast of the power plant, its tall, immense stacks etched against the moon. It marked the outskirts of the city. He pulled himself up on the tire, his chest resting on it, to give his arms rest. For the moment he was content to let the current take him where it might. Ahead of and behind him the river was empty, and he had the sudden feeling he was the only human left in the world, a drifting castaway swallowed up by the night and the vast, lonely waters. The cold had made his arms and legs numb, and now his mind seemed to be going numb too, as though if he did not concentrate, he might fall asleep or slip out of his body and be lost among the faraway, glittering stars.

A night heron screamed from the bank, startled him off the

tire and broke the spell. He began to scan the bank for a place to land. He thrashed his legs to restore circulation in them. When the current brought him within a few yards of a wooden point, he let the tire go and swam for shore.

He clambered up a low clay bank and immediately began to shiver. He waved his arms, slapped his shoulders, and walked in a circle to warm himself. The tire drifted away, and soon he lost it in the shadows from the trees along the bank.

He had made it out of the city.

Turning away from the river, he stepped into the woods, still cold and shivering.

CHAPTER SEVEN

A woodpecker's hammering awoke him. The sky was gray and overcast. He had no idea what time it might be, but judging from the hunger pangs in his belly it must be well into the morning, he reckoned. He rose from the creepers and undergrowth where he had slept and took a quick inventory of his pockets. The matches were not good after his swim. His billfold contained only the soggy banknotes he had taken from the woman, and the two snapshots of Peg and Suzie which had remained dry in the plastic sheaths. He had no food. The only weapon he possessed was his pocket knife. He was in great shape, he reflected, for survival in the boondocks.

Yet, he had escaped the city—which was more than poor Ross had done. He knew he should feel grateful for his luck.

Through the trees in the distance he could see a levee. He decided to take a chance and climb it for a look around. When he reached it, he found that it was higher than he thought, maybe thirty feet with a steep grassy slope, and stretched apparently for miles in both directions like some gigantic Indian burial mound, and as forlorn and desolate.

He climbed it and peered cautiously over the top. Below, on the other side, lay the flat, treeless delta as far as the horizon with row upon row of soybeans as far as the eye could see. A twenty-foot chain mesh fence topped with barbed wire cut off the field only a few yards from the levee, and a dirt road ran on both sides of the fence. From the fence came a slight hum. Anyone attempting to cut through it or climb it would get a nasty, possibly lethal, shock.

Rankin gaped at the vast sea of bean plants in amazement.

There was in front of him enough beans surely to feed hundreds of thousands of people; yet the government claimed constant food shortages. But much of it was being swapped overseas for raw materials to use in exotic weapons, and more was being kept in silos and grain elevators. By controlling the food, the generals controlled the people.

His own hunger gnawed at him, and he clenched his fists in helpless anger.

Far down the road between the fence and levee a dust plume headed toward him. He scuttled back down the levee and into the woods. He had seen four armed soldiers in the jeep ahead of the dust cloud.

He decided to follow the woods south along the river. Although he had no real idea yet where he wanted to go, he intended to put as much distance between the city and himself as he could. As he walked, he caught occasional glimpses through the trees of the river. Once he spotted a patrol boat skimming up the middle of the river on its hydrofoils, too far away for him to worry about.

Later on in the afternoon, he came across some wild muscadines and gorged himself. An hour later, he had stomach cramps so violent they took his breath away. It was nearly dark before he felt well enough to push on.

A light shone through the darkness and, as he approached, became a window in a tin-roofed shack that stood on stilts several feet above the ground. From where he stood on a rise, Rankin looked in the window and saw a lantern-jawed man, a worn-looking woman, and two kids eating at a rickety table. He pictured himself knocking on the door and asking for a handout. There was no TV antenna on the roof; they seemed to be too poor for TV. Yet, even if they did not recognize him as an enemy of the state, they would probably be suspicious of a stranger, and he dared not take any unnecessary risks.

But behind the shack lay a bedraggled garden. He sneaked into it and grabbed two tomatoes, then slipped back into the woods. As he ate a tomato, he thought of a story he had read once in school about a monster, Grendel, who lurked in a swamp and, because he was an outcast, raided the surrounding countryside and struck fear into the inhabitants.

Rankin grinned mirthlessly as the tomato juice, like blood,

ran down his chin. He was an outcast, all right, but he lacked the fearsomeness or strength of a Grendel.

Some time in the middle of the night he came to a ramshackle structure on stilts near the river's edge. A rusted metal sign over the sagging gallery read, "Dooley's Bait Shack. " A dirt road led down to it from the direction of the levee, and a little way up the road sat a darkened two story frame house. At the river bank, tied to a willow tree, he saw a small rowboat.

He walked up to the gallery on a long plank and tried the door, while peering through the glass pane into the dark, cavernous interior. The door was locked. He broke part of the pane in the left hand corner with his elbow. The glass fell and shattered on the floor inside. He reached in, turned the lock, and let himself into the pine-smelling interior, loud with the singing of crickets. He let his eyes adjust to the gloom and, from the moonlight streaming through a dust window, he made out seines and hoop nets hanging from the wall like cobwebs. In shallow wooden boxes along one wall and covered by screens the crickets shrilled. Above them, on a shelf, were cartons of styrofoam cups with holes punched in the lids for the night crawlers. Moving over to a dust wooden counter, he found some of what he was looking for: packs of fishing line and plastic boxes with various-sized hooks. He pocketed some of both and also a couple of packs of matches he found in an ashtray. On second thought, he emptied one of the plastic boxes of hooks and stuck a pack of matches in it to keep them dry. He began to look around for guns and ammo and anything to eat. But, as he passed the rear window, he saw a light go on in the house up the road.

He cursed softly and waited. Then he heard the front door of the house close and a dog bark. It was the first one he had heard in a long time, and it came as a shock. He sprang across the room and onto the gallery. He teetered down the plank on a dead-run and heard a voice booming from the house: "Get 'em, Buster! Go get'em!"

Rankin jumped from the board and began to run along the bank. It was too late to try to steal the boat, he thought, as he stumbled through the underbrush. He had forgotten that, in the country, some people might not have had to eat their dogs. Behind him the dog barked again—much closer than before. He shot a quick glance behind him and saw a long, dark shape streaking toward him. The dog looked huge in the moonlight and, in another few moments, it would be on top of him.

A few feet away the water glimmered. Rankin jumped in and began to swim away from the bank as hard as he could, praying the dog would not follow. Behind him, he heard it barking and snarling from the bank. He turned and saw the dog running back and forth along the bank frenziedly. Behind him, a flashlight bobbed as a man came running toward him. Rankin took a deep breath and went under the surface, still swimming hard.

When he came up, he was already out of range of the flashlight, but he was afraid his head would be a target in the moonlight, and he promptly dove under again. This time, when he surfaced, he spotted a drifting log nearby. He swam underwater and came up behind it. He could no longer see the man or dog against the curtain of black trees, only a tiny circle of yellow light as it moved back and forth over the water from the bank.

Rankin clung tightly to the slick log and wondered if he was destined to be forever on the Mississippi River without a boat.

The island loomed ahead of him, its trees a black, shadowy mass against the night sky. The current carried him down the side facing Arkansas. He could see its low shoreline three-quarters of a mile across the water. For nearly an hour he had held onto the log. Now he abandoned it and swam for the island, aiming for a fallen tree that projected from the bank into the water less than fifty yards away. But the current pulled him past it and carried him another two hundred yards before he managed to reach the bank and grab some overhanging vines. He hauled himself up the clay bank and lay there face down, panting and exhausted. At last, shivering in his wet clothes, he got up and wandered through the trees and creepers until he came to a little clearing.

He felt in his pocket for the plastic container with the matches, debating on whether to build a fire. But, finally, he decided against it for fear somebody might be on the island or that somebody on the relatively close Mississippi shore might see and become suspicious of even a small fire. He would have to spend another shivering night in wet clothes.

Like an animal he circled the small clearing looking for the softest spot on which to curl up and sleep.

CHAPTER EIGHT

At sunset Rankin looked out over the river from a thicket and watched a string of barges go past. Two guards with laser guns stood talking with a deckhand on the bow of the towboat. He watched the tow until it disappeared down the river beyond a bend. His first day on the island had been a long one; more so since he had found nothing to eat.

At daybreak, he had risen stiff and cold to explore his new domain. It had not taken long. In half an hour he had covered the island from top to bottom and found he was the only human being on it. Although thickly wooded, it was less than two hundred yards across at its widest point, and perhaps half-a-mile long. The rest of the day he had devoted vainly to finding something to eat. There were squirrels and birds, but he had nothing to catch or kill them with and, then, there were the catfish in the river.

He had turned over a rotten log and had found plenty of fat slugs and grubs clinging like barnacles to its underside. He had used them for bait, impaling them on the hooks he had stolen. He had tied the lines to bushes along a quiet little inlet where a log lay wedged against the bank at a forty-five degree angle, then resumed his hunt for food. He had hoped to find at least some wild berries to take an edge off his hunger, but it was too late in the year.

Several times during the day he had checked the lines, rebaited some of them, moved some of them to other likely looking places, but he had caught nothing but some chiggers in the brush. He was beginning to take a dislike to his new refuge.

The sun dipped slowly behind the Arkansas shore and streaked the sky the color of blood. He rose from the thicket to check his lines once more before it got too dark. But, again, he found nothing. He needed something rotten for bait like bird innards that had festered in the sun for a couple of days to attract catfish. Badly discouraged, he wandered back to the clearing where he had spent the previous night. As things stood, he might wind up eating the slugs and grubs he was using for bait. Soon, it grew almost pitch black. A cold breeze came from the river. To cheer himself and ward off the chill, he decided to build a small fire and, in a short time, had a blaze going.

Watching the dancing flames, he thought of Peg. She had always loved campfires and the smell of burning leaves. He tried to picture her as she had looked in those days, but try as he might, he could not bring her face into focus; it remained a misty shadow in the back of his mind. He had never before had trouble conjuring up her face and suddenly he felt a stab of panic. For the moment, it was as though she had never existed and that he had only imagined her. He pulled out his wallet and gazed at the snapshots of her and Suzie in the flickering light.

They had told him while he was recuperating in a veteran's hospital on Long Island. Even though, by then, he was accustomed to death, he had not believed it —not at first. Later, when he had come home and saw the crater where the apartment building had been, he believed. They were gone—the feisty red-haired woman he had cared more about than his own life, and their eighteen-month-old daughter that he had never seen again after being air-lifted to England a year earlier and would never see grow up, go to her first dance, have beaus, become a woman.

A mist swam before his eyes. He put the wallet back in his pocket and stared at the flames. Overhead the leaves sighed in the breeze. An owl hooted dismally.

He made up his mind he would not stay on the island for long.

Maybe he could steal a boat and, like Huckleberry Finn, drift down the river. If he could reach New Orleans, he might sneak aboard a foreign freighter bound for Australia or Brazil. Australia was still free, they said, and in Brazil nobody gave a damn who you were or where you came from or why. But, even as he thought about those places, he realized the chances of getting aboard a ship bound for anywhere or even getting to New

Orleans were remote.

A chill began to pierce into his vitals. He stirred the fire with a stick. It began to die, but he did not feel like feeding it any more. He found himself thinking of Sam Ross, not with bitterness, but a kind of detachment. Clearly, the skinny teacher must have been mad when he posted up his crazy document. What the hell good had he thought would come from doing such a thing? It had simply gotten him killed. But, in the end, he had faced death bravely, allowing Rankin to escape.

Looking at the dying fire, he wondered if it might not have been better if he had been killed with Ross four nights ago. He shook his head and decided the solitude and night were beginning to get to him.

After a while, the fire flickered down to embers. He poked the embers with the stick and sent a shower of sparks cascading upward. He threw the stick away and settled down on the ground to sleep.

Nearby, in the brush, he heard a shrill squeal—the death cry of a rabbit caught by an owl.

CHAPTER NINE

The skiff with three armed men emerged out of the morning mist. One man in the bow had an antique Springfield strapped over his shoulder, and another carried a shotgun. The third man rowed across the muddy water in short, choppy strokes that propelled the skiff surprisingly fast. Now, Rankin could make out the bearded face of the man in the bow with the Springfield. It was quiet and purposeful.

Rankin scrambled backward in the brush, rose to his feet, and headed toward the other side of the island as fast as he could go. Maybe somebody had seen his fire last night, or maybe they were playing a hunch after his raid on the bait shop, or maybe they were only hunters. But it did not matter who they were if they found him. And the island was small enough that it would only be a matter of time before they did. He had been checking one of the lines he had set out when he heard the car or truck motor over on the Mississippi side. The sun was not yet up, and a thick, white mist obscured the shore less than a quarter of a mile away, but he had been instantly alert for any sound of a boat coming from that direction. Within five minutes after the motor had been shut off, he heard the muffled sound of oars approaching through the mist. He had moved down the bank in the direction they seemed to be coming from, keeping himself carefully concealed. Then the boat had suddenly appeared, a dark shape in the mist.

Rankin plunged through a thicket and was confronted with the river again. He had reached the other side of the island. The Arkansas shore was too far for him to swim to and, if he ran ahead of them up the island to the farthest end, he would probably have at most only a matter of minutes before they flushed him out. He could try to circle back to the other side of the island and swim the four hundred yards to the east bank, but already the mist was beginning to lift. If they saw him, he would make an easy target in the water.

There seemed only one other choice. He slipped into the water and swam a little way toward the foot of the island. After a hundred yards or so, he emerged from the river and began to double back across the island toward the skiff. Every few yards he stopped to listen for the slightest sound of their approach. His nerves were taut, but his perceptions seemed heightened. He saw every leaf beneath his feet and every twig—sharply and distinctly. Thin filaments of cobweb glistened from the bushes in the gray, milky light.

Somewhere to his right, a mockingbird trilled and, when it fell silent, Rankin thought he could hear his own blood pounding in his temples. The mockingbird started up again—then ceased abruptly. Rankin froze. He waited for the bird to start again. When it did not, he sank down on his belly in the brush.

The man seemed to materialize out of the gray dawn light gradually, like a Polaroid snapshot developing in front of Rankin's eyes. First, he was only a blurry outline, then he became solid and, finally, Rankin recognized the bearded man in the bow, only now he was peering intently at the ground, and the Springfield was unslung and cradled in the crook of his arm. He was barely fifty feet to Rankin's right and, behind him, a bigger, bald-headed man appeared with a shotgun. The bald man veered off to the right, head bent like the bearded man. From time to time both of them looked around sharply. Rankin pressed himself tighter against the ground.

Suddenly the big man motioned to his companion and pointed forward.

Rankin knew they had found his trail. He no longer had the slightest doubt as to their purpose on the island. They were after him.

The two moved quickly and silently in the direction Rankin had first fled. Where was the third man, Rankin wondered. He was the joker in the deck. The two others would reach the Arkansas side of the island in a couple of minutes and double back. It might take them a minute more to figure out what he was up to, but not much more. At most, he should have no more than three or four minutes headstart.

Rankin rose and stumbled toward the skiff. He cursed his leg for slowing him down. First, it had taken away his high-steel job and made him a night watchman, now it might cost him his life. He stopped to pick up an oak limb, then plunged on. An oak limb against a rifle and shotgun and whatever the third man had—wherever he was. His breath came in short pants now, and sweat began to drip into his eyes.

As he approached the place where he had watched the skiff, he stopped to gain control of his breathing. Then he crawled forward, eased the brush aside, and saw the skiff tied to a willow tree. The third man sat in it facing the bank. He had a stub of cigar clenched between broken teeth, a cobra tattoo on one forearm, and a dirty red bandanna tied around his head. Beneath beetling brows he had small yellow eyes slightly slanted like a cat's. He fingered a machete that he held between his knees and, in his belt, was a ten-inch hunting knife.

Slowly Rankin withdrew a few feet into the brush, picked up a stick, and threw it behind him in a line with the boat. He waited a few moments and tossed another one in the same direction. Then another.

He heard a scraping sound from the boat. Then brush crackled as the man came up the bank.

Again, Rankin pitched a stick, a heavier one, at the same place. He crouched behind a sweet gum and gripped the oak limb more firmly.

Move, damn you—move, Rankin thought.

Silently, with the machete poised, the man passed six feet from the sweet gum in the direction Rankin had thrown the sticks. The heavy oak limb caught him on the forehead. He dropped instantly. The machete skittered into the brush.

From behind him came a whistle—one short note, followed by a longer note.

Rankin dropped the limb and ran for the skiff. Pulling out his pocketknife, he sawed the rope that held the boat to the willow. In another moment he clambered into the skiff, grabbed the oars, and began to pull away from the bank.

From the brush came a groan, then the man he had hit staggered onto the bank, clutching his head, his eyes wild. The hunting knife seemed to suddenly appear in his hand. But Rankin had already pulled the boat into the current, and the other dropped rapidly away.

"You gimpy sonuvabitch, " he snarled at Rankin. Then he began to yell. Moments later, another yell sounded close behind him. Rankin threw himself into the oars with every ounce of strength he had. Soon he would be out of shotgun range, but not of that ancient Springfield which had been standard issue for American combat troops in a long, forgotten war. Yet, it was still deadly. He pulled hard.

The mist had completely vanished, burned away by the sun, which meant he was a sitting duck if he did not get more distance between himself and the island. Then, what he dreaded, happened. He saw the stocky man joined by the other two.

The bearded man dropped to one knee and pointed the Springfield at Rankin from three hundred yards away.

Rankin let go of the oars to fling himself face down, but suddenly a hot, flashing pain seared through him.

The impact knocked him backward into the bow and, for a moment, he was gazing at sky through a red haze. Another bullet slammed into the stern. Splinters of wood flew around him. He lay on his back, dazed and numb as the haze gradually cleared. In the distance came the crack of the Springfield once more. He felt the warm flow of blood running down into his shirt.

He looked and saw that the bullet had hit him in the left shoulder. Strangely, he did not feel much pain now. He struggled up so that he could peer over the side of the boat, and saw that he was drifting past the foot of the island. He pulled in the oars with his right hand. A bullet sent a little spray of water against his hand and, a moment later, he heard the rifle's report. Soon he would drift out of range of that bearded bounty hunting bastard.

Still lying on his back in the bottom of the boat, he ripped off part of his shirt. He wrapped it under his armpit and around the wound, using his teeth to hold the end of the strip while he tied the knot with his good hand. He raised his head and gazed at the oars. He could not row with one arm against the current. He was completely at the mercy of the river; he could only go where the current directed.

Yet he needed to get ashore.

It would not be long before the bounty hunters swam the channel to the Mississippi side, got back to their car or truck, and came after him. They did not look like the type to notify the authorities. They would want the full reward. They would try to get another boat or get to a point ahead of him on the shore and ambush him.

But, before that, a patrol boat might come along and finish him.

He peeked over the stern. He was drifting around the bend, and it shut the island from his view. No more islands, he thought—you could be too easily trapped on one.

His shoulder had begun to throb sharply. He shifted his weight to ease it, but it continued to feel like somebody was prodding him with a white hot poker.

CHAPTER TEN

He watched the trees and bank slide by, trying to ignore the throbbing pain in his shoulder. He had to reach the bank. He turned around facing the bow, stuck the right oar into the water, and tried to pull toward shore with one arm. Against the strong current he made little headway. The bank remained tantalizingly close but out of reach.

Ahead was a creek. Clenching his teeth against the pain, he dug the oar deep into the water and soon was drenched with sweat. But it was no good. The mouth of the creek, half-concealed by thick overhanging vines, slid past, and a big mud turtle sunning itself on the bank blinked at him with beady yellow eyes.

Rankin quit rowing. He was panting with exertion. He had only two alternatives—to either swim for shore or drift helplessly and soon be picked off by the bounty hunters or picked up by a patrol boat. He decided to swim. But first he had to rest.

Although the bank was only a hundred feet away, he was not sure he could reach it with one arm against the current. The sun had risen above the trees now and glared off the muddy water. Overhead, a big crow flapped toward the Arkansas shore and cawed in derision as it went by. Rankin watched the crow fade to a tiny speck. He began to feel lightheaded. The blood had soaked through his makeshift bandage and was seeping down his rib cage. If he did not strike out for shore quickly, he would either faint or become too weak to have any chance of reaching it.

He shook the cobwebs from his brain and eased himself over

the side. He clung to the stern for a minute letting the chill water wash over him. Then he struck out for a dead oak downstream that jutted out from the bank into the river.

But the current carried him beyond it. He felt himself growing weaker and knew he could not swim much farther. He went into a dead man's float. When he brought his head up, the boat was much further from him than the bank. Again, he stroked and made some progress, but his strength ebbed rapidly. The thought came to him that he was going to drown. He began to flail with both arms, and the pain from the wounded shoulder made him gasp. Yet now, the bank was close—very close. Only a few more strokes—one, two, three—and he would reach it. He went under and came up again choking, flailing, his hands clawing for the muddy bank. He grabbed a thin vine and tried to climb up the bank, but the vine snapped and water closed over his head. As he went under, he thought he heard the snarl of an outboard motor.

When he came up, he saw everything through a blur—the bank and the thin vines he clutched, the boat beside him, the black face bending toward him, strong hands that grabbed him beneath the armpits, causing him to scream in agony as they hauled him up from the water into the boat. Then he passed out.

There was a strong smell of fish. Also a smell of gasoline. He became aware of a buzzing sound that he gradually recognized as the sound of an outboard motor. Trees glided by overhead, mingling their cool shadows with dappled sunlight. He turned his head and stared into the cold, bulging eyes of a big catfish. He tried to get up. In the stern of the boat, a man watched him, his broad, dark face impassive beneath the brim of a leather cap. He did not have a gun that Rankin could see— only a large hunting knife in a sheath at his belt.

As he sat up, he felt a sharp twinge in his shoulder. He sank back, his head propped against the bow seat and saw that they were moving up a creek with dense underbrush along both banks. Vaguely he wondered where they were going—probably to a place with a telephone.

He wondered too why the black man had not cut his throat. Maybe he had not recognized him or maybe he would be content with only half the reward that came with turning him into the Sepos.

Rankin wanted to struggle, to jump out of the boat, to do something to resist. But he was too weak and in too much pain.

He felt, when he moved, the whole side of his shirt stick with blood against his ribs. A tiny breeze from their motion fanned his face, and the shade from the overhanging trees cooled his feverish body. He waited for the other to speak. But the man continued to stare at him without expression. Rankin noticed that there were several large catfish in the boat before he slipped again into oblivion.

A bearded man with eyes like a ferret pursued him through a dark sewer. Try as he might, Rankin could not outrun him. At last, he turned to face his pursuer. The bearded man raised a rifle—its mouth gaped as black and sinister as a snake hole at Rankin.

He cried out. A black face peered into his own. He felt something cool on his shoulder then the black, shrivelled face of the woman disappeared.

He was in the river again. The current kept pushing him away from the bank that he struggled frantically to reach. Finally, he reached it. A slender dark-haired woman—it was Lucinda Burke, he thought—reached out to grab his hand. She pulled him up the bank with one hand. Suddenly she moved the other hand from behind her back and started to stab him with a long ice pick.

Rankin groaned. The shrivelled face of the black woman reappeared hazily. He strained to bring it into sharper focus. The face was ancient, a maze of wrinkles, a mummy-like face with red-rimmed, rheumy eyes that stared intently at him. The woman lifted something off his shoulder and then put something else back on it. She nodded at him silently and left.

He fell asleep again.

Through a narrow slit in the curtain made from a Ralston Purina feed sack, sunlight streamed across his face. He blinked, squinted, then tried to sit up, but winced and settled back on the pallet. He was in a small room that smelled strongly of woodsmoke and was sparsely furnished with, besides the pallet, a chair, and a battered old trunk. The walls were unpainted, adorned only with a few faded color photographs and a calendar with a picture of a waterfall beneath a bridge.

For some time he lay on the pallet in a dream-like, but not

unpleasant, trance and watched the streak of sunlight creep slowly across the pallet and onto the wall. He heard no noise beyond the closed door of the room. He idly wondered where he was, but it was enough for the moment that he was alive and not in some Sepo headquarters.

Finally, however, he summoned his will, heaved his legs over the side of the pallet, and rose shakily to his feet. He felt dizzy, his legs rubbery. With one hand against the wall, he launched himself across the room. Next to the door hung a fragment of mirror. He froze in front of it, and a scarecrow face, with the spiky beginnings of a beard, wavered in the slightly distorted glass. The sunken eyes had dark circles. As he stared at the specter of himself, the door opened. A dried-up mummy of a woman, with the wizened face he had thought he dreamed, stood before him. The red-rimmed eyes in the black face held an expression of amusement.

"You feelin' well enough to admire yourself, I see. " She chuckled.

Beyond her he could see into the other room, glimpsing a table, fishing seines on the wall, and two pegs for a rifle or shotgun. But there was no gun.

The old woman continued to regard him with a kind of secret enjoyment.

"When my son brought you here, you weren't so lively, no sir. Now why don't you just get back into bed. 'Cause if you fall down, I ain't big enough to pick you up again. "

"How long have I been here?"

"Two days. And out of your head some of the time. But I put poultice on you and your fever gone now. Get back into bed. " She took his arm and guided him firmly to the pallet. He sat down on it.

"The bullet passed clean through you. But you lost lots of blood. That's why you be so weak. Now lie down like I tells you. I don't wanter be messin' with having to pick you up off the floor. "

"Where's your son?" Maybe he had gone to report him to the Sepos.

"He be back after a spell. I 'spect you hungry now. I'll go get you something to eat. "

After she left the room, Rankin thought about running. But run to where? He did not even know where he was. And his journey across the room had left him exhausted. He pulled the window curtain back and looked outside. Wherever he was, it was in the woods. Beyond the edge of the clearing for the house, rose an unbroken wall of trees as far as his eyes could penetrate.

The old woman returned. He did not even know he was hungry until he took the first spoonful of warm broth. It tasted like fish, was lightly seasoned, and delicious. He attacked it.

She watched him, her wrinkled face somber now, but attentive.

When he finished the broth, he thanked her. She took the bowl silently and started out of the room. At the door, she turned and told him to get some more sleep. He watched the streak of sunlight gradually fade from the wall, replaced by the shadows of the trees, and wondered if the son would return with Sepos. But maybe neither the man nor the old woman had recognized him. If they had and planned to turn him in, it would not make sense to tend his wound and feed him broth, he reasoned.

Voices came from the other room in a low murmur, but he could not distinguish the words. It was twilight outside. In the glimmering light from the window the fragment of mirror shimmered like a dim moon. Outside the door were heavy footsteps, then the man entered the room. At first, Rankin could only see the whites of his eyes clearly in the gloom and his broad outline.

He crossed the room and stood over Rankin's pallet, staring down. He said nothing. He seemed to be weighing something as he studied Rankin.

"Seems like I caught a big one with you, " he said at last. His voice was deep but curiously gentle in such a powerfully built man, thought Rankin.

"Thanks for pulling me out of the river. "

"When I seen you was shot, I almost threw you back. "

The odor of cooking food wafted from the other room.

"And thanks for tending me. "

"Three men come across me yesterday in my boat. They were lookin' for you. "

"What did you tell them?"

The other sucked his teeth. "I told 'em I seen somebody like you rowin' over to the Arkansas side the other morning. "

Rankin struggled up into a sitting position. "I won't trouble you any longer. "

The Negro pushed him back down so easily Rankin felt embarrassed. He had no doubt now that the Negro knew who he was—bounty hunters, that could only mean one thing.

As though he read Rankin's thoughts, the other laughed. "You wonderin' why I ain't turned you in for a big reward. And you probably thinking I didn't tell them three 'bout you so I could have the whole reward myself. "

"Yes, " Rankin admitted. "Why didn't you turn me in?"

The big man looked away from Rankin and gazed somberly out the window at the fast falling dusk.

"I got my reasons, " he said finally. "Now I got some chores to do. There's one thing though. " He bent close to Rankin and spoke very softly and matter-of-factly: "If anybody happens to find you here, I'm gonna have to kill you and tell them you just that moment broke in. "

He rose and walked out of the room.

Later in the evening the old woman appeared and gave him another bowl of broth. She brought a kerosene lantern, set it on the trunk, and he ate by its glow. Some time afterward the man appeared, smelling of whiskey and carrying a pallet. He set the pallet down a few feet from Rankin's, snuffed the flame out in the lantern and, after undressing, flopped down on the pallet with a groan. Soon he was snoring heavily.

Rankin wanted to leave, but he knew he was too weak to get very far As long as somebody from the outside did not discover him, both he and his hosts would be safe, he guessed. But he did not doubt that, to save themselves, they would kill him, just as the man had said. What other choice did they really have?

CHAPTER ELEVEN

The old black woman, Esther, changed his bandages regularly and coated the wound with a kind of paste she made from herbs and plants she picked in the woods.

"Some folks uster laugh at me 'bout my cures, " she told him. "Most of um dead now. "

Her foxy reddish eyes studied the new bandage she had applied. She nodded, apparently satisfied. "Soon you be choppin' wood with that arm again. "

She straightened up. Next to her, on the wall, hung a framed color photo of an athletic-looking young black. She noticed Rankin's gaze and turned to the photograph.

"That's James, my grandson. "

"Looks a lot like his father, " Rankin remarked. The boy had the same broad face and strong chin, the same penetrating gaze as Esther's son. "Where does he live?"

Her face took on the impassive expression her son habitually wore.

"I don't know. "

She turned and left the room.

Rankin had been with them for three days now, and he had learned little more than their names and what Jason, the man, did for a living. He hunted and fished, and the old woman had a vegetable garden. Sometimes, he peddled some of his catch using an old, dilapidated pickup truck to carry the buffalo, bass, and catfish into town several miles away.

He had a shotgun which he carried in the truck, and an old .38 Ruger that he left with the old woman. Rankin felt sure she was under instructions to shoot him if somebody should discover him in the cabin. When she tended him, she left the pistol in the other room, a nicety Rankin appreciated. He could have overpowered her and taken the pistol, but had decided against it. He planned to leave shortly and, anyway, he owed them something. Jason had possibly saved his life and, in sheltering him, they were running a considerable risk. For the hundredth time he wondered why they bothered.

That evening after supper he and Jason sat at the table in the room that served as kitchen and living room as well as bedroom for Esther, who slept in an old-fashioned brass bed against the far wall, adorned with a beautiful patchwork quilt. Curtains over the windows were drawn.

Jason worked a plug of tobacco meditatively while Esther cleaned dishes down at the creek. They might have been living in the last century, Rankin thought, since there were no modern conveniences like running water or electricity. It was quiet and peaceful here, and he felt a little envy. They had vegetables, all the fish they could eat and any game Jason bagged with the shotgun.

"Pretty good hunting around here?" he asked.

Jason lit a kerosene lamp, checking again to make sure the curtains were drawn tight. He blew out the match, replaced the glass chimney, and watched the flame rise as he adjusted the wick.

"It's a good day when I get a rabbit or a couple a squirrels, " he said tonelessly. "These parts 'bout been hunted out. "

His face gleamed like an ebony mask in the glow from the lamp.

"That's still more meat than anybody but the rich get in the city, " Rankin said. "And, if you get a deer even once a year— "

Jason's tobacco-stained teeth showed in a bitter smile.

"I ain't seen a deer in two, maybe three years. And, Mister, I been all over these bottoms. "

He got up, took the shotgun down from the wall, went outside, and returned a couple minutes later with a jug of whiskey. Replacing the shotgun on the wall, he sat back down at the table and poured some of the clear moonshine into two glasses and handed one to Rankin. They both drank. Tears sprang to Rankin's eyes. The whiskey seemed to sear all the way down into his belly.

Esther came back with the dishes and put them up, except

for an old coffee cup. She came over to the table with it, and Jason poured a liberal dram of whiskey into the cup. Rankin was amazed to see her drink it down in one gulp without even blinking.

"I'm goin' ter bed now, " she announced.

While she undressed, they went out and sat on the wood-pile. Jason refilled their glasses. For a long time they drank in silence, Jason moodily, Rankin enjoying the peacefulness of the night. Down at the creek a frog sang. Rankin felt easy.

"How did you come to live here?" he said at last.

"It was my grandfather's. When they took away my farm, I come back here. "

After the war, the government had appropriated the small farms and combined them in the name of efficiency into the kind of huge plantation Rankin had earlier seen at the levee. But, Rankin suspected, the real reason they had done it was to more strictly control the food supply at its source.

"Them three white men that were lookin' for you, " Jason poured himself another slug of moonshine, "I didn't like their looks. They looked like buzzards. You could tell by their eyes that they wanted to find you real bad. What all did you do?"

Rankin told him.

Jason said nothing. They heard a splash as a fish jumped in the creek. It was completely dark now and the moon had not yet risen. The peaceful mood Rankin had felt moments ago had vanished. The three bounty hunters might return and find him here and, if they did, Jason and Esther would be in the middle of a very bad situation.

"Why are you helping me? You know you could get a lot of money for turning me in, and you know the risk you're running by not doing it. "

"That's right. " Jason took another drink from his cup. Rankin helped himself to the jug.

"But that would be doin' something for them. " Jason almost spat the last word out. He stared down at the dark water of the creek.

"You're helping me because they took your farm?"

"I worked my guts out to get that place and to make something of it—something to be proud of. But that ain't the reason. "

He might have been carved from the wood itself, motionless as an ebony idol perched on its woodpile throne.

"They took my boy. " He spoke so low it was like a whisper.

Instantly, Rankin recalled the color photograph of the boy that looked like Jason.

"One reason my wife and I worked so hard on that farm was so we could send him to college. His first year there, they had one of them student protests against the government. They say he was one of them that marched. The police arrested him and some others. "

"When?" Rankin said.

"Right after the war. I ain't heard from him since. I went to the police and they wouldn't tell me nothin'. Him and those other students—it's like they don't exist, like they never was. " Jason got up from the woodpile and went down to the creek. He stood there a long time. When he returned, Rankin told him that he planned to leave early in the morning.

Sleep eluded him. His thoughts were on the morning and what he would do, where he would go. He could no longer go down the river since he could not row. Maybe he could steal a car and stick to the back roads. Driving only at night and staying away from towns he might avoid road blocks and checkpoints. But there was always the problem of gasoline. Without a ration card and an identity card, as soon as he reached empty on the fuel gauge, he would have to steal another car, and then another. Three or four stolen cars might get him to New Orleans if Sepos, bounty hunters or ordinary law abiding citizens did not get him first. He needed a gun.

Before dawn, Esther rose and fixed a hot breakfast on the cast-iron woodstove. After they ate, she changed Rankin's bandage again.

"You lost too much blood to be travelin' so soon, " she muttered. "You think I done tended you all this time so you can fall on your face out in the woods and rot?"

"I'll try not to rot. "

"I think you're a bigger fool than you look. " Her red eyes were angry, but her fingers were gentle.

She gave him a jar containing the same greasy salve she had applied to the wound and told him to continue using it for the next several days. He pulled out the banknotes and put them on the table. They were wrinkled from the river.

"What's that for?" she demanded.

"Man, you insultin' us. " Jason said, scowling. "We don't want your money. "

"It's not my money. And I'm not paying you for what you've done for me because I can't. "

"Then what's that for?" He was still indignant and so was she.

"Because it's come to me that I don't have any use for it. What am I going to do, walk into a store and buy something with it? Maybe a new pair of slacks or a wrist watch? Or, how about a pack of cigars or some aspirin?" He shook his head. "If you don't take it, it won't be any use to anybody. Hell, if you don't want it, burn it. "

He turned to go. Behind him, he heard Jason's footsteps and his arm blocked the door.

"I can take you down the river a piece if you want, " Jason said.

Rankin could not let him run any more risks. He shook his head. Esther handed him a paper sack with some food in it.

He looked at her ancient, wrinkled face and then at Jason's calm, impassive one. He wanted to say something, but could think of nothing. Instead, he grasped each of their hands for a moment. Then he was out the door.

He crossed the clearing away from the creek. In a few moments the trees shut out the shack, and he was alone in the dim woods with the scent of wet pine needles. He did not look back.

CHAPTER TWELVE

He kept to the woods as much as possible. Esther was right. He found he was too weak to walk very far at one time, and he had to pause often to rest. Much of the day he spent hiding and resting in a deep thicket. Once he saw a hunter crossing a field less than a hundred yards away from where he lay, but the man disappeared into a large copse of trees. He was the only human Rankin saw all day.

Toward dusk he came to the edge of an empty field. Beyond the field lay a shabby collection of houses and buildings and, above them, loomed a rusting water tower. He bided his time, waiting for darkness, and ate the food Esther had packed. The village had a peculiar main street. There were buildings only on one side of it and their fronts faced Rankin. On the other side, nearest Rankin, ran a railroad track parallel with the street. A dilapilated boxcar stood on the tracks and several small kids played around it. But, by the time the few street lights came on, the kids had left.

When it was completely dark, Rankin left the shelter of the trees and crossed the field to the boxcar. He crawled up in it, conscious of a slight pain in his chest. From the open door he could see Main Street barely stretching two blocks and consisting mainly of crumbling brick one-story buildings. Sandwiched in the same building between a pool hall and drugstore was the hardware store. All the businesses were closed and dark except the pool hall. Rankin cursed. It would have to be right next to the hardware store. All he could do was wait now until the pool hall closed. Through its lighted window he saw a figure bent over one of the green felt tables and another leaning on a cue stick.

The yokels around here would go to bed early, probably even the ones at the pool hall. If he were lucky, he would not have to wait much past ten or eleven. He counted the vehicles on the street. There were only seven, and three of them were pickup trucks. All of them were ancient, dating back well before the war. He noticed one of them had two flat tires.

He watched impatiently the dim figures move around the pool tables. Now he could see several more people who must have emerged from a back room. They were drinking beer, and the faint strains of country music drifted out onto the street. His chest still ached, and it seemed hard to breathe. Just tension, he thought. Once he started moving, the tension would leave and adrenalin would take over; he would get a gun and a car and be on his way. But, he would have to wait until the town was asleep and, right now, that meant the yokels in the pool hall.

A paper cup rolled fitfully up the street, propelled by an occasional gust of breeze. He amused himself by wondering if the cup would reach him before the pool hall closed. It did and continued fitfully past him toward the darkness beyond the edge of town. It rolled out of his sight, disappearing into the night.

Gradually, the pool hall began to empty, and the antique vehicles on the street dwindled in number until finally only the one with two flat tires and a scabrous red Mercury remained. But the owners of the Mercury seemed content to shoot pool and drink beer all night. He watched the moon climb over the rusty water tower.

At last, two men swaggered out of the pool hall—one thin, one heavy-set, both wearing levi jackets and broad-brimmed cowboy hats. Under a street light they circled each other, fists raised in mock combat. One, the heavy-set man, feinted a kick. The thin one rushed in and grabbed him around his bull neck. Both of them lost their hats, and Rankin could see their faces clearly, young and hard and slightly drunken.

"Leggo, you sonuvabitch, " said the stocky one.

"Ahh, piss on you. " His companion turned him loose, picked up his hat, brushed it carefully with his elbow. He looked up and down the empty street and his horse face had a petulant expression. "Let's find some action. " He adjusted his hat carefully on his head.

The other retrieved his hat. They both got into the Mercury, the engine rumbled, and they roared away leaving a haze of exhaust fumes in their wake.

Soon afterward, the pool hall proprietor, a bald, withered man, turned out the lights, locked the door, and walked away up the street. Rankin saw him turn a corner and disappear down a side street.

He waited another half hour, then climbed down from the boxcar and crossed the street. He ducked down a narrow alley and approached the rear of the hardware store. The back door was fastened outside by an old, dented padlock. He was getting good at breaking and entering, he thought. He could hear the low sound of thunder far away.

In the blackness of the store he groped around and blundered into things, until finally he had to strike a match. He searched for a gun rack and, failing to find that, he looked for the glass counter displaying handguns. There was none. He ransacked drawers and boxes and swore under his breath. He had spent all that time in the boxcar waiting in vain. This jerkwater store did not carry one gun, not even a B.B. gun. He had to content himself with a hunting knife he found in a display case with jack and pen knives. He stuck the hunting knife, sheathed, into his belt and left the store the same way he entered.

A few yards behind the store ran a five-foot high chicken wire fence. Beyond the fence were darkened houses shrouded by trees. The moon had vanished behind dark clouds and the breeze was stronger, bringing the smell of rain. Rankin followed the fence until he found an empty metal drum that he used to climb over it. He walked through a backyard and came to a one-story frame house with a carport. The house was dark and silent. He padded softly to the carport where an old foreign sub-compact was parked. Even in the darkness, he could tell it was ready to fall apart. And, anyway, it was too close to the house. By the time he got it started, if he could get it started, the owners would awake and be on top of him.

He headed up the street toward the edge of town. A few of the houses he passed had cars, most did not. But the cars were parked too close, like the first one, to the houses. At the outskirts of town, he came to a pickup truck parked along the edge of the road. Like the other vehicles he had seen, it was old and battered, but it was separated from a flimsy frame house by a wide ditch full of stagnant water. A long plank lay across the ditch. Rankin looked at the dark house, then peered up and down the road. He pulled the plank up and laid it along the side of the road; he tried the truck door facing the road, and it opened with a groan of rusty hinges. He ducked down behind the steering wheel. The windshield was cracked, and he did not doubt that the engine block might be too but, taking a deep breath, he decided to give it a try. He fumbled under the dash and found the ignition wires.

In the distance thunder rumbled—a storm was drawing closer. As he worked, he kept glancing at the shack. He touched the right wires, and the engine turned over sluggishly, sputtered, died. He tried again, and suddenly a light came on in the house across the ditch. The motor sputtered again, coughed, almost caught. Gritting his teeth, he tried once more. The door to the shack flew open, a man appeared on the porch in his underwear, a big man.

"What the hell you think you're doing?" he shouted.

He started off the porch. Rankin held the wires together and muttered a steady stream of oaths. Headlights appeared in the rearview mirror from an approaching car. For an instant, the man stopped at the edge of the ditch, but he hesitated only an instant, then he floundered through the water toward Rankin. He stood out in the glare of the on-coming lights and, in one hand, Rankin saw he held an iron pipe.

Rankin straightened up in the seat as the engine roared into life. But the man climbed out of the ditch and lunged for the passenger door. Rankin open the door and with all his weight against it flung it back, catching the other in the chest but, at the same moment, he saw the man's eyes widen in recognition. Then he toppled backward into the ditch.

Rankin shoved the truck into gear and jammed his foot down on the accelerator. The truck jerked forward and the engine almost died, but he coaxed it back and began to pull away. Behind him the man staggered out of the ditch and stumbled into the middle of the road. He chased Rankin several yards, abruptly stopped, turned, and began waving his arms at the car that was almost on him.

In the rearview mirror, Rankin saw the car screech to a stop, and the man run over to the driver's window.

He pushed the accelerator to the floor. Behind him, the car started up again, leaving the man still standing in the middle of the road, waving his arms.

Rankin was certain the man had recognized him in the glare of the car's headlights and that he had told whoever was in the car, but the driver was not going to share the reward. The truck was up to sixty-five now and shimmying all over the road. He gripped the wheel tightly and concentrated on staying on the asphalt.

Ahead of him he saw a side road, braked hard, and skidded onto it, then accelerated again. The road was gravel, the truck had no shocks, and he bounced all over it from one side to the other. Behind him, in the dust, he could make out like twin dim moons the headlights of his pursuer. He had the truck up to seventy now, as fast as it would go, and his heart was clenched like a fist. Any moment he expected to crash into the trees on either side as he fought to stay on the road. The car was gaining on him.

His gaze flicked to the speedometer needle that was glued on seventy. He could not push another mile-per-hour out of the truck, his foot already was against the floorboard. His eyes burned as he stared out into the darkness beyond the splintered windshield. He kept the lights off in the hope that he would somehow yet elude whoever was behind him. The road ahead was straight as a plumbline and the trees on either side now gave way to flat fields. As the car's headlights drew nearer, Rankin decided to take a chance and to try the advantage of the truck's four-wheel drive. He eased the wheel to the right and, in the next heartbeat, had spun off the road into the field. His head struck the roof of the cab as the truck jolted and jerked across the furrowed field like a badly animated cartoon character. At the end of the field he could make out a black tree line.

Suddenly a tire blew and the truck swerved crazily. He fought to keep control; the steering wheel was almost wrenched from his grasp as he continued bouncing over the furrows toward the trees. He noticed behind him the car had turned into the field and its headlight beams shot up and down as it crossed the furrows. There was no longer any hope of escaping his pursuer in the truck. The car closed rapidly.

He was near the trees now. He allowed the truck to glide to a halt. He flung open the door and dashed for the trees.

Just before he reached them a bullet sang overhead and snapped off branches and twigs ahead of him. He dove to the ground and crawled into the trees. As he reached them, he turned in time to see the car skid sideways to a stop beside the truck. Two men piled out, and one of them held a rifle.

Lightning lit the whole field in sharp, eerie relief, showing the pickup with its ruined tire, the scabrous red Mercury beside it, and two figures in wide-brimmed cowboy hats—the same pair he had seen under the street lamp outside the pool hall— running toward him.

"It must be him, Darrell, " cried the stocky one. "He was limping. It must be him all right. "

Thunder drowned out Darrell's reply.

Rankin crawled under a rusty barbed-wire fence and worked his way deeper into the pines. Then he got to his feet and began to run. But soon he had to slow down. His chest ached; his bullet wound hurt. He was, indeed, he thought, a sorry physical specimen.

Gather 'round ladies and gentlemen! He walks, he talks, he limps, he gimps, and there is a price on his head. Ain't it wonderful that our government will pay for this mangy, grubby, sad piece of work such a bountiful amount. So try your hand, ladies and gentlemen, at bagging this puny feller, pitiful as he is—it's open season. Yessir! Step right up!

Rankin grinned sardonically.

Overhead lightning flashed, thunder crashed.

Let's find some action, the horse-faced cowboy had said. He should be happy now, Rankin thought as the first drops of rain spattered around him. He pulled out the hunting knife from its sheath and plunged ahead. Abruptly, the trees ran out, and he slid down a bank onto a dirt road.

He darted across the road. The bank on the other side was a tangle of kudzu vines. Struggling up the bank, he found himself in a field covered with the lush vines. They had strangled a big oak and its white skeletal branches were stark against the dark sky. He had to rest. He sank down into the kudzu a few feet from the oak, his eyes straining to penerate the darkness across the road.

In a stab of lightning, he saw them standing on the opposite bank and staring down the road. The skinny one held the rifle. They had come through the woods fast.

Rankin burrowed down deeper into the vines and gripped the hunting knife more tightly. His fear was almost so palpable he could smell it like the supercharged ozone in the air. Again his eyes tried to penetrate the darkness across the road, but he could see or hear nothing. The rain began to pelt him hard and, in a few moments, rivulets were running down the back of his neck.

A flash of lightning revealed the bank across the road was empty. Had they retreated back through the woods or were they in the road preparing to come up into the kudzu? In a moment he had his answer. As soon as the clap of thunder passed, he heard a voice in the road.

" . . . Ain't goin' up there, Darrell. I ain't. "

"But you can see his footprints here in the dirt. He's up there, damnit, " Darrell whispered.

"Yeah, and maybe he's got a gun. And there ain't any trees to cover us up there. "

"He don't have a gun, " hissed Darrell.

"How do you know he don't? Can you say for certain?"

No reply.

"I didn't think so. Look, let's go back to town and get some help. "

"And split the reward money with a bunch of others? No way. I'm goin' up there, " said Darrell. "He don't have no gun. "

"Then you're goin' by yourself. I don't have a gun either. "

"Go on then, you chickenshit bastard. But you ain't gettin' none of the reward neither. "

Then followed silence. Rankin strained his ears to pick up another sound from the road, but he heard only the rain on the kudzu and the hammering of his heart. He waited a long time. Across the road the tops of the trees thrashed in the wind. Suddenly, in a lightning flash, he saw just a few feet from him the crouched figure of Darrell advancing slowly, cautiously—his lean horse face, pale and strained, the rifle's muzzle pointed at a spot almost directly over Rankin's head. In another moment he would be directly on top of him. Every muscle in his body went taut. A foot brushed against his arm.

Rankin sprang up, slicing with the knife in a quick short arc.

The cowboy screamed and collapsed into the vines with a severed hamstring. He clutched between his crotch with both hands. Rankin stopped and picked the discarded rifle up from the vines. It was a .22 semi-automatic. He crashed the butt of it down hard against the other's skill.

He bent and satisfied himself that Darrell was still breathing. Then he went through the man's pockets. He found a jack knife, a pack of chewing tobacco, and a box of .22 long shells. He pocketed the shells and stared a moment at the drawn, unconscious face turned up to the rain. He placed the cowboy hat over it.

I guess you found enough action for one night, he thought.

He hurried away as quickly as he could through the thick vines that clutched at his ankles and feet, while the rain poured down and thunder rumbled overhead like the end of the world.

CHAPTER THIRTEEN

From the trees Rankin watched the boy playing with a plastic yellow boomerang. He lay on his belly and tried to ignore the pain in his chest that had become constant now. Beside it, the discomfort from his shoulder seemed minor. He coughed.

The trailer gleamed in the late afternoon sun. There was an old pre-war sedan parked beside it, which meant there was somebody in there. The trailer sat on a hill surrounded by woods with no other dwelling in sight. He was waiting for dark. Before dawn he had dropped from a railroad trestle onto a slow-moving log truck and ridden for twenty miles before he had to swing off when it turned into the rutted yard of a country sawmill. All day he had walked, taking more and more frequent rests the weaker he became, until he had stumbled onto the trailer. He knew he could go no further without food, water, and perhaps medicine and a car. When darkness came, he hoped to obtain all of them at the trailer. He wished he knew how many people were inside it and if they had guns.

The boy, about seven or eight years old, had emerged from the trailer fifteen minutes before. He seemed greatly amused with his boomerang, because he threw it tirelessly. Sometimes it came back to him, and he would attempt fancy catches behind his back and between his legs; sometimes it did not return and he had to run and retrieve it. This time, Rankin watched it sail far out over a steep gully, arc lazily, then plummet abruptly into the gully bank and roll down it.

From his vantage point, he saw it come to rest at the gully bottom, and he saw something else. Two dogs emerged from the brush and ghosted along the bottom of the gully. Both were big and gaunt, the one in the lead was a dirty, yellowish color, the other charcoal black. Something in the way they moved, bold yet furtive, alerted Rankin. Then they stopped.

The boy started into the gully. He was halfway down the bank when he saw them and froze. The yellow dog bared its teeth and went for him. Its companion followed.

Frantically the boy scrambled up the bank and started for the trailer.

Rankin could see he would never make it. Already the yellow dog had reached the top of the gully and would bring him down before he was halfway there.

Rankin nestled the .22's stock against his cheek, sighted on the yellow dog, took a breath and exhaled part of it. In the Army he had qualified as an expert marksman, but he had been out of practice a long time, had never fired this rifle, did not even know if it was sighted correctly, and his target was moving fast a hundred yards away.

The boy looked back and screamed.

The dog sprang at him and seemed to swim before Rankin's eyes as he squeezed the trigger. The dog spun in mid-air and collapsed. The black dog raced past its companion and launched itself at the boy; the rifle cracked again, and the dog fell on its side, struggled back up, and Rankin fired gain. The dog jerked, fell back over, and remained motionless.

The boy whirled around and gazed at the two bodies. He looked toward Rankin, his face ashen. A woman rushed out of the trailer and ran to the boy. She stared at the dogs, knelt, and grabbed the boy to her. The boy looked toward Rankin again, and she followed his stare. No one else had emerged from the trailer. He decided to take a chance.

He rose and started toward them—his eyes on the trailer windows, alert for any movement inside. The pain in his chest made it hard to breathe. He coughed again.

The woman stood up as he approached, one arm still around the boy's shoulders. Her green eyes watched Rankin warily. Her glance shifted from his face to the gun and back to his face.

"Who are you?"

She was in her thirties, wore jeans, and an old sweatshirt, smeared with paints.

"The one that kept him, " he glanced toward the boy who was looking again at the yellow dog, "from being dinner. "

She looked at the dogs and shuddered. In death they had a more wolfish aspect. The yellow one had been shot in the head, a lucky shot indeed, he thought, since he had aimed for its body. The black one had been hit in the hind quarters and the chest.

"I'm grateful, " she said at last. But she still eyed him warily. He could not tell whether she recognized him.

"Is there anyone else in the trailer?"

"Why?"

"Is there?" he rasped.

She shook her head and held the boy tighter.

"I need water—and food." He felt sweat break out on his forehead. "I need water right now. " The woman and boy blurred for an instant.

"What you need is a doctor, " she said. Her voice sounded far away. "You're sick. "

His vision cleared and he motioned them toward the trailer. They walked ahead of him and it was hard for him to keep up. With each step he felt like he was walking in heavy sand but, at last, he reached the trailer door. He blinked and sagged against the trailer wall. He did not think he could climb the trailer steps. The sun seemed to dim, the rifle slipped from his grasp, and he sat down on the steps. He blinked again, and the woman held the rifle pointed at him. She ordered the boy to go inside and he obeyed.

The rifle pointed at Rankin's chest did not waver, nor did her eyes from his.

"If you're going to shoot, do it. Or else give me a drink of water. "

"I don't want to shoot you. Don't make me. "

He laughed raggedly. "Fine. I won't make you. Now could I have a drink of water?" His tongue felt thick. The woman did not take her eyes off him.

She called the boy and told him to bring out a glass of water. When he did, she told him to go back inside.

"I want to get my boomerang. "

"Don't argue with me. Do as I say. "

Reluctantly the boy started inside. From the doorway he gazed down at Rankin.

"Is he the man on TV?"

"Jeff!"

The boy disappeared inside. Rankin drank the glass of water.

He set the empty glass on the ground and looked at her. She had high cheekbones and shoulder-length brown hair.

"So, you do know who I am. "

"I do now. I wasn't sure at first. "

"What decided you?" he said bitterly. "Let me guess. The limp, right?"

He saw the answer in her eyes. He could have grown a beard like Rip Van Winkle, even had plastic surgery, but the limp would betray him still.

"Well, what are you going to do?" he said.

"I don't know. " For a moment her eyes flicked toward the two dead carcasses. "What were you doing in the woods? You were watching us, weren't you?"

He nodded.

"Why? What did you plan to do?"

"Get food and water. Steal your car. " He saw no point in lying. Again she seemed to blur in front of him. Suddenly he longed to be in the woods again, to lie down in the pine needles and sleep. When his eyes focused clearly on her once more, her jaw was set, her green eyes were hard and steady.

"I want you off my property and I want you off quickly. " She motioned him up with the gun barrel. He got to his feet, a fever chill ran through him.

"On your way! Before I call the police. "

He walked slowly toward the woods. The trees wavered in front of him. He hoped he could make it to them without having to rest. He felt the weight of the woman's gaze on his back. From the trailer's back window he glimpsed the boy watching him too. He reached the trees, leaned awhile against a gum tree, felt for a moment as if he would collapse, but the moment passed, and he shuffled deeper into the woods. He wondered vaguely why she had decided to let him go. Grateful, he supposed, for saving her son from the wild dogs. But, he did not ponder her generosity long. He wished it had extended as far as giving him back the rifle, but he told himself he ought not be greedy. She might change her mind yet and call the cops, he thought, and he headed deeper into the woods. The trees seemed to revolve slowly one way, then the other.

He was standing on a merry-go-round. Suddenly he was sitting. He shut his eyes to make the spinning stop. He shivered and thought of Sam Ross. Ross had had a fever, the old fugitive fever. It seemed to go with the territory. You couldn't be a genuine state enemy without it. He coughed, lay down on his side shivering, and curled up into a fetal position for warmth. But soon he was sweating again. He got up, took a few steps, stumbled, and slid into a little ravine, landing on his wounded shoulder. Blood began to seep through his shirt, but he did not particularly care.

Sleep—he needed sleep. He shut his eyes and saw bright, hypnotic eyes staring at him. At first they seemed to be the yellow dog's, but they were too bright—they had to belong to the hophead dwarf with the ice pick. He opened his lids to rid himself of the vision, but the eyes were still there staring down at him. They widened at the sight of the growing blood stain on his shirt, but she still held the .22 rifle on him steadily.

You changed your mind, he thought, and decided to finish me.

She stared at him for what seemed a long time from the edge of the ravine. Slowly she started down toward him.

CHAPTER FOURTEEN

Motionless, he waited as she slid down the side of the ravine. Then she was standing next to him. He grabbed her ankle and yanked. She sat down abruptly, and he pushed her shoulders to the ground. She struggled, one hand clawing at his face— the other still clutching the rifle. Then she let go of it and shoved her palm against his wounded shoulder. He gasped, cursed, and struck her in the face.

She became still and stared up at him, eyes blazing. He reached for the .22 and noticed the canteen beside it. He rolled off her and sat gasping for breath. His eyes went from the canteen back to her. He picked it up. It was full.

She sat up and dusted the dirt and leaves from her arms. "I thought you could use it. "

He tried to get to his feet and help her up. But he was too exhausted and sank back down again leaning on his elbows. His shoulder throbbed.

"I thought you meant to shoot me. "

"I still might, " she said flatly.

"I've got the gun. " But the truth was he could barely lift it.

She reached over and took it away from him. "Now you don't. " She set it down.

A glint of anger still lingered in her eyes. But she lifted her hand and felt his forehead. Her hand was cool. She smelled of paint, turpentine, and woman.

"You're burning up. " She unscrewed the top of the canteen and lifted it to his lips. Water dribbled down his chin. She took a handkerchief from her pocket and soaked it, then put it to his forehead and began to mop off the sweat.

"Why?" he said.

"Because I must be crazy. " Her hand on his face was gentle now—the same one that a minute before had jammed against his shoulder. Her face in repose had two vertical worry lines right above the bridge of her nose which was slightly crooked, but delicately shaped with a small arch. Her cheek was still flushed red where he had struck her.

"I'm sorry I was rough with you. I didn't know— "

"Didn't know what? If I'd wanted to shot you, I could have done it from up there. " She nodded toward the top of the ravine.

"Lady, any time I see a gun, I figure I'm the target. "

She said nothing, but took the handkerchief away, poured some more water on it, then placed it back on his forehead. Her eyes rested on the blood stain. She began to unbutton his shirt. The vertical lines above her nose deepened.

"What happened?"

"I was shot. "

"Who wrapped it?"

"An old black woman. "

"It may be infected. That could be causing your fever. "

He shook his head. He had faith in Esther. He told her his other symptoms.

She said it sounded like pneumonia, that her sister had had it with the same symptoms. She bit her lower lip thoughtfully.

"I'm going to have to redress your wound. I don't know what to do about the fever. I've got some antibiotics at home from when Jeff had the flu a few weeks ago. I'll check with the doctor. " She saw the alarm in his eyes.

"I said I'll check. I won't bring anybody. "

Picking up the rifle, she climbed up the ravine bank.

"I'll be back. "

He watched her disappear into the trees.

The fever gave him a curious floating sensation occasionally broken by chills and coughing. He hoped there were no more wild dogs lurking nearby. She had taken the rifle. She did not trust him, and he was not sure he trusted her, but it really made little difference. Even if she planned to come back with the police, he felt too weak to leave the ravine. Nearby a dove mourned. It was growing dark. A chill gripped him and his teeth chattered. He curled up again in the fetal position. In a little while he began to sweat again.

The woman was back, kneeling beside him. It was still twilight. She gave him two white pills to take.

"Penicillin. " She put the canteen to his lips.

He swallowed them with the water.

She took the bandage off his wound and grimaced—then began to clean it. Her hands were firm, yet gentle.

"You ever done this before?"

She shook her head. "No. And I hope I'm doing it right. "

Amen, he thought.

After she had rebandaged the wound, she sat back on her knees and wiped her forehead with her wrist.

He started to lie back down, but she shook her head. She told him that with pneumonia he was not supposed to lie down, because fluid would collect in his lungs.

"So I'm supposed to sleep sitting up?"

She nodded.

"I can't. I never could. "

"Yes, you can. And you will. "

"Easy for you to say. You will be in your warm, comfortable bed. " Suddenly he thought that with a son she must be sharing the bed with a husband and wondered if the husband knew about him. He glanced at her ring finger and saw the plain gold band. She saw his glance and must have read his thoughts; a faint amusement showed in her eyes.

"We're separated, " she said. "Nobody knows about you but Jeff and me. "

He noticed that she still had the rifle beside her. It rested on top of two rolled blankets. She put the rifle aside and unrolled the blankets.

"They smell like moth balls. But they ought to keep you warm tonight. " She met his gaze. "I can't take the chance of having you in the trailer. You understand? It's not just me. I have my son to think of. "

"Yes. "

She rose. "I've done what I can for now. I'll check on you later tonight to see how you're doing. " She started away, then turned. "There's one thing I need to know. I hope you'll tell me the truth. "

"What?"

"Have you killed anybody?" Her eyes studied his intently.

"No. "

She nodded, apparently satisfied.

"Did they say I have?"

"On TV they said you badly wounded a man—with a knife." Her gaze flicked to the hunting knife at his belt.

"Did they say he tried to kill me—with the gun you're holding?"

She looked at the rifle in her hand. "No. "

"I didn't think so. " He thought about all the others—the Sepos that night in the barge depot, Lucinda Burke, the man with the baseball bat in the slums, the dwarf, the three bounty hunters who had damned near succeeded—besides the skinny pool hall cowboy. They all seemed to blur together into one—a dark, terrifying composite with no face, only a blind, raging lust for his blood.

When his gaze turned outward again, she was gone. He had not even heard her go up the ravine.

He sat with his back against the bank. Above him, the leaves whispered in the wind and through the trees he could see a few stars. The dove mourned again. He coughed and his chest felt like it would crack open. Rankin wondered if he would die here. It was, he thought, a better place than the sewer. The rustling leaves were oddly comforting. After a while the ache in his chest eased a bit.

He slept fitfully—sliding back and forth between a comatose wakefulness and dark, weird dreams. He sweated beneath the blankets, removed them, then pulled them back over him after a prolonged rigor. He dreamed he was in a coffin. He kept trying to get out and they kept pushing him back down. Nearby yawned an open grave, a mound of raw earth beside it. They carried the coffin to the grave and began lowering him into the earth.

He awoke, threw off the blankets, and started scrambling up the side of the ravine. When he was almost to the top, he lost his footing and slid back down. He had a sharp pain in his chest and he gasped for breath. A sob tore from his throat, and only then did he realize where he was—in the ravine and not in some graveyard. He sobbed again, but with relief. Yet, as he looked up at the sky, he still felt like an animal trapped in a pit and, for a moment, he felt panic roar through him and a crazy urge to climb out of the ravine and run. After a fit of coughing, he started to crawl up the bank, his fingers clawing at the soft earth.

He reached the top and lay on his back panting.

"What are you doing?"

She stood before him, no longer smelling of paint and turpentine, but faintly of perfume. She still toted the rifle, however, like she was beginning to like it.

"Climbing out of that damn ditch, " he said. "It gives me the creeps. "

"I guess there's nothing like exercise, " she said dryly. "I thought I told you not to lie down. "

"What are you—my den mother?"

But he heaved himself up into a sitting position. She squatted down beside him and handed him a small cylinder of tablets.

"I went into town and got these. The doctor is a friend of mine. Take two right now. "

"What are they? "

"Big medicine. Now quit stalling and take them."

He swallowed them dry, because he had left the canteen down in the ravine.

She produced a small thermos. "Nourishment!" Her face was a pale blob in the gloom, and he smelled the scent of perfume more strongly. His teeth began to chatter. She opened the thermos and steam rose with the odor of chicken noodle soup.

He was not hungry, but she insisted he take a sip. Then another. At least, he thought, it warmed him and made his teeth stop rattling together and helped the pills go down. She put the top back on the thermos. "I got it out of a can. I didn't know you were going to be so particular. You can have the rest later. Are the blankets warm enough?"

He nodded. "Did your boy get his boomerang back?"

"Yes. " In the darkness he could barely see the smile, then it faded. "I took him into town with me. When we got back, he insisted on going into the gully. So I went with him with a flashlight and—the rifle. We found it all right, but the dogs were gone. I had dragged their bodies, " she shuddered at the memory, "into the gully earlier, but they were gone. I guess some tramps got them and took them away—for food. "

For a minute they were silent. Her hand rested on the .22.

"The man you got this from, " she said, "is he the one that shot you?"

"No. " He told her about the three bounty hunters on the island. She asked more questions, and eventually she had most of the story in bits and pieces. He never mentioned, however,

Jason and Esther by name or where they lived. When he finished, she did not speak for some time. The wind stirred her hair. She sat motionless beside him, the rifle on the other side of her, her hand still resting on it. The moon had risen, and its light, filtering through the rustling leaves, made shifting patterns on her face.

She was, he thought, a lovely woman and her closeness and the subtle scent of her perfume almost made him forget how bad he actually felt. Her husband must be a fool to let her go.

She turned to him at last. "Where do you plan to go? What will you do?"

He told her about Australia, and she shook her head impatiently.

"Even if you get to New Orleans, do you think you can just walk onto a ship? Don't you know they're always watching for that very thing?"

She was right, of course. But he had to hold on to something, even if it was a pipe dream. She seemed to sense this because, when she spoke again, her tone was softer.

"I have to get back to Jeff now. You're supposed to take those pills every four hours. " She rose, paused, and gazed down at him. "Will you be all right?"

"Yes. "

She nodded, but still lingered.

"So, you were going to steal my car. How far do you think you could get in your shape?"

"Farther than if I walked. "

"I guess so, " she agreed. "Well, goodnight. "

She walked quickly away through the trees toward the trailer. When she was out of sight, he turned to the place where she had sat beside him. The .22 still lay there, its barrel gleaming faintly in the moonlight.

CHAPTER FIFTEEN

Somebody was shaking him. "Wake up!" The woman's face was close to his.

"What?" he muttered. He sat with his back against a pine tree near the ravine.

"Get up!" she ordered. "Quick!"

"What is it?"

It was still almost dark; he could barely make out individual trees close by.

"You've got to get up. People are coming—they're hunting for you. "

He stared at her. The ache in his chest was dull and persistent.

"They've moved the search into this area. It was on TV. Somebody thought they saw you only half-a-mile from here. It must have been a tramp, but they thought it was you, and now they're combing the woods. You've got to go. Hurry!"

He grabbed the .22, threw off the blankets, and tottered to his feet. In the gloom her eyes seemed enormous. "Go where?"

"I don't know, " she said. "But you've got to get away from here. "

Of course, he thought. He was only a few hundred yards from her trailer. He looked around. "Do you know which way they're coming?"

"From town, " she pointed east. "It's only three miles from here. " She laughed, but there was a ragged edge to it. "My father called from town a little while ago and told me to watch out for you and keep the doors locked. He said the Sheriff and deputies would be out here soon and then I'd be safe. Safe!" She looked around wildly. "Please, will you go now?"

"Yes. Take your blankets—and thanks."

He started weaving his way through the trees away from the direction of the town. He had a curious sensation of being outside himself and watching himself. He also felt as if he were floundering in wet sand. He had covered less than fifty yards when he heard the footsteps. He kept going. She ran up to him.

"You're staggering like a drunk. " She sounded angry. "You won't get a quarter-of-a-mile. "

"Yes, I will. Get back to your trailer. "

Her face was very pale. "Oh, God!"

He started away. She reached out and grabbed his arm. "Wait! I know this place a few miles from here. "

He watched her mouth form the words and push them out. They came out fast, and he only half-registered them. " . . . take you there . . . got to be at work soon . . . but I can take you there . . . we have to go right now . . . "

With her pale, strained face and the rushing words, he suddenly felt sorry for her. She was frightened and seemed slightly crazed. He started past her, but she held tightly to his arm.

"Look. You still think you owe me something for yesterday, " he said. "But you don't. Now get back to your son. "

"They're going to kill you. You think you can fight or run? You can barely walk, and a child can take that rifle away from you. They're going to kill you. "

"Thanks for the confidence. "

"I'm not going to let it happen again. I won't stand by and do nothing. Not again! You hear me?"

He stared at her. What the hell, he wondered, was she talking about?

Although she was still pale, her jaw was set and her eyes looked determined.

"We're wasting time. They could be here any minute. " She scanned the trees anxiously. "I'll bring the car to the edge of the woods. Can you make it that far?"

"Maybe. "

"Maybe, hell!" She took his arm and pulled it over her shoulder. "Move, damnit! Move, you bastard!" She hurried him toward the edge of the trees.

She left him in nearly the same spot where he had lain yesterday afternoon when he had shot the dogs. She ran inside the trailer, reappeared a few moments later, got into the sedan, cranked it up, and swung it toward him.

A few moments later he was lying on the back floorboards between the seats, as they bounced down the rutted drive. Then they were on a gravel road going fast. Gravel pinged off the underside of the car. She was silent for several minutes. Once, she turned and looked at him a moment, her face still pale but calm. She turned her gaze back to the road. The sky had become gray now.

"This place, " she said. "It's an old tumbledown shack by the swamp. My cousins and I used to play in it when I went to visit them as a child. I took Jeff out there last summer when we first came back here, thinking it would be gone, but it wasn't. It's almost completely overgrown, and I think we were the only ones who had been down there in months. "

She slowed the car a few minutes later, cut the wheel sharply, and the trees closed above them like a tunnel. He raised up and peered out the windshield. The trail, little more than two ruts in the earth, descended gradually and was choked with weeds. On either side vines and creepers snaked down from the trees. A damp, earthy smell clogged his nostrils. Ahead of them lay a wide pool of water surrounded by black mud. A pickup truck or jeep might get through it, but not the sedan. She braked the car and got out.

"Wait here. " She skirted the water and disappeared around a bend in the trail.

In less than five minutes she returned and motioned him to get out.

"It's okay, " she said. "I don't think anybody will find you down here. The shack is just around the bend. But I warn you, it's pretty grim. A little way in back of it you'll find a spring. I'll try to bring you some food tonight. " She gave a short, nervous laugh. "I'll be late for work. Do you think you can make it to the shack by yourself?" Her face had regained its normal color.

He nodded.

He watched her get into the car, start it, and back up the trail toward the gravel road. When she was out of sight, he started down the trail. He skirted several mud holes, rounded the bend, and there was the swamp. It stretched as far as he could see. Grassy hummocks rose here and there out of the dark water along with hundreds of dead trees. The bleached trunks loomed like pale ghosts above the rising sun.

To his left, he saw the shack with its rusted sagging tin roof and gaping windows. It was half-smothered in vines and creepers. He sat down and rested a little while, listening to the frogs and watching the sun draw off the mist from the swamp. He reloaded the .22, replacing the three shells he had used on the dogs yesterday. The woman had taken a big chance driving him out here. If they had run into a roadblock or if she had been seen letting him into the car even, it would have been all over for her as well as him. She had known that and yet, frightened as she was, had taken the chance anyway. Why? She had brought him water, food, and medicine because he had saved her son's life, he had thought. But there was something else behind it, too, he realized now.

"I won't stand by and do nothing. Not again!" she had said.

Another chill gripped him. He pulled out the medicine she had brought him and swallowed two more of the white pills. Then he got to his feet and walked slowly toward the shack.

Whoever built it must have craved privacy badly, he thought, to locate in such a desolate place. Probably a moonshiner, definitely a swamp rat.

The door hung crazily by one hinge. He shoved it back. A fat spider scuttled across the broken plank floor, and the odor of rotting wood blended with the rank smell of the swamp. There were two windows, both with shattered panes.

Home, sweet home, he thought. It was completely empty except for the spiders, rat droppings, and a piece of stove pipe that curved down through the roof and hung in mid air like a periscope. It was not the Grand Hotel, but he had been in a couple of worse places recently. He went back outside and sat on a cinder block that served as the doorstep. Like all abandoned places, the shack seemed to exude a melancholy that seeped over him like the swamp mist. After awhile, he decided to go look for the spring she had mentioned.

He found an overgrown path behind the shack and followed it for a hundred yards into the woods. In a tiny, moss-covered clearing a clear pool of water bubbled up and spread for several feet. He knelt, cupped his hands, and drank. It was cold and he drank greedily. He could not seem to get enough. Finally, he sprawled on his belly and drank with his lips to the pool. The water was so cold it hurt his chest when he swallowed, but he kept on until he had gotten his fill. Then he lay on his back and gazed up at the sky. He liked this place and he did not want to return to the shack.

A slight breeze stirred the leaves on the trees overhead. The leaves were beginning to change. By now it must be October, he thought. Soon enough cold weather would come and winter would arrive.

He wondered if he would live to see the winter.

After awhile, he got up and made his way slowly back to the shack.

She came after dark bringing blankets, two small tins of meat, a jar of peanut butter, bread, a thermos of hot soup, and a bar of strong soap. The latter, she told him, he needed more than the others. He took the soap and went to the spring muttering to himself. When he came back, she handed him the thermos top full of soup.

She rubbed a finger on the floor. "I should have brought a broom. "

"Shall we go outside, madam?"

"Karen. I also brought you this. " She handed him a flashlight.

They sat under an oak a few yards from the shack and watched the moon climb over the swamp. By moonlight it seemed less bleak. He asked her if the police had come to the trailer.

"If they did, we weren't there. I took Jeff to school and went to work. We're staying with Dad in town. He doesn't want us to stay at the trailer as long as . . . "

"As I'm on the loose?"

She nodded. "And also because of the wild dogs. I had to tell him about it. I told him a hunter shot them. He asked me if I knew the man. " She looked at him, her eyes luminous in the moonlight. "Of course, I told him you were some passing stranger. He said I was lucky you came along. " A trace of mockery twisted her mouth.

"He never wanted me to live out in the boondocks. He wanted me to stay with him after Chuck and I separated and I came home last summer. "

"You're pretty isolated out here. "

She wanted the freedom to be alone and paint in her spare time, she said. A friend of her father's owned the trailer and the land it was on and rented it to her.

He remembered the paint on her clothes when he had first

seen her. "What type of pictures do you paint?"

"Mainly things out of my own head—fantasy."

She smiled. "I guess it's an escape from . . . the way we live, all of us. Drink your soup. "

They were silent for a while and he finished the soup. Around them the frogs sang. He asked her if the separation was permanent and did she plan to get a divorce.

"I don't know. " She stared out over the swamp and her eyes seemed to cloud. "He says he wants us back. We were married when I was twenty. I thought I knew everything, including him. And of course, I didn't. He doesn't drink or run around with other women, it wasn't that. In some ways he's a good husband. And I hurt his career"

A shape flitted past them so abruptly, yet silently that only after it was gone did Rankin realize it was a bat. She was still staring out over the swamp and apparently had not noticed it.

"How did you hurt his career?"

"You ask a lot of questions. " She felt his forehead with a cool hand. "Your fever seems down. Are you taking your pills?"

"Religiously. What does he do?"

"He's an aerospace engineer at Huntsville. "

He asked what she did here. She told him she was a secretary at a shoe factory, and that before, in Huntsville, she had been an art teacher. Her voice had a bitter edge.

"Did you like it?"

"I loved it. They made me quit, and I'll never be able to teach again, of course. "

He stared at her. "Why not?"

She told him. There had been a regional art contest for the high schools. Her best student had submitted a charcoal drawing which she had entered in the contest. One day, two men in suits and ties came to visit her. The student who had drawn the charcoal picture was taken out of school and sent to a special center for "reorientation, " and she had been "asked" to resign immediately.

"What was the picture?"

"It was simple. Three people—a man, woman, and child— seen from the back, gazing through a barbed wire fence at a field of ripening corn. The people were thin. "

The bat swooped low over the swamp feeding on mosquitoes.

"I hear they're teaching my course with a computer now, " she said. "Painting by the numbers. My student who was sent to reorientation came back before I left. He doesn't draw or paint any more. He told me he planned to go into tool and die work. He was very enthusiastic about it. "

"They took away your career for that. " The government had taken away the job she wanted to do, and an exploding rocket in Manchester had ended forever any chance of him doing again the high steel work he had wanted for the rest of his life.

"They took Chuck off a highly classified project he had been working on right after that. We had some bad quarrels after he was demoted to a smaller, non-secret project. He kept asking me over and over how could I have sent such a picture into the contest—didn't I know it was subversive? I kept telling him it was not only the best picture, but it was honest. " She shook her head. "Honest! God, I should have known better. "

"You wouldn't do it again, then?"

She looked at him sharply. "Would you help that teacher again, if you had it to do over?"

He did not answer.

She rose. "I've got to get back. Dad thinks I'm doing some late work at the office. I made Jeff promise not to mention you to him or anybody else. Jeff isn't positive who you are, but I think he had a pretty good notion. "

"Kids are pretty sharp. "

"Were you ever married?" She smiled. "On TV they say you're single. "

"Yes. I was once. "

"What happened?"

"She's dead — and our daughter. "

"I'm sorry. " She touched his shoulder. In the moonlight her face was still. "Do you want to talk about it?"

No, he did not want to talk about it. And then, to his amazement, he was not only telling her about Peg and Suzie, but how he had felt for years afterward and how he still sometimes felt; he told her about drifting and drinking, about working at meaningless jobs that had petered out or that he had quit after only a few weeks until, at last, after one drunken binge that had lasted a week, he had finally gotten hold of himself, eventually landed the watchman's job at the barge depot, and had decided to try and make the best of his situation. She listened intently. After he had finished, he felt oddly relieved, as if a weight had somehow been lifted, at least temporarily. He had never told anyone before the things he had just told her. He wondered why he had now after all these years.

She did not speak for a long time, just looked at him. Then she put her arms around him, embraced him briefly. "Take care of yourself, " she said.

She turned and walked away up the trail toward her car. He watched her slender form recede in the moonlight.

A mosquito bit him on the back of the neck. He slapped it and looked at his palm. When he gazed up in her direction, she was gone.

Two days passed, and he did not see her again, or anyone else. Physically, he had begun to feel better. The chills and fever subsided, the ache in his chest lessened, the cough weakened and became less persistent. The medicine was doing its job. He began to explore and discovered a small, shallow lake not far from the shack. He tried fishing there for a couple of hours, but he had no luck.

On the second night, after she had brought the flashlight, he took it and, with a sharpened stick, went frog gigging. After an hour and several misses, he speared a big bullfrog, went into the woods, built a small fire, and ate frog legs. He went back to the shack, hoping she might show up, but he had no good reason to expect she would. It would be risky and foolish for her to return—they both knew that. He told himself he was a selfish bastard for wanting to see her again. He slept under the old oak where they had talked, instead of inside with the spiders. Wrapped in the blankets with the .22 beside him, he slapped mosquitoes until he finally fell asleep.

When he awoke the next morning with a dozen mosquito bites, he decided it was time to clean up the shack. He found some old rags beneath it, soaked them in swamp water, and cleaned up the rat turds. He swept away most of the cobwebs and evicted some of the spiders. With pine needles he swept up part of the dust and rearranged the rest of it. Feeling vaguely righteous after these efforts, he went up to the spring with the bar of soap and took a bath for as long as he could stand the icy water. Then he washed his clothes. While they dried, he sprawled naked on the moss in the warm sun with the .22 within easy reach and gazed up at the soft blue sky through the webbed branches of the trees. High overhead a gray squirrel tightroped out on a narrow limb of a sycamore and stopped to survey his next move.

Slowly Rankin raised the rifle and drew a bead on him. He could have squirrel for breakfast. But he did not pull the trigger for fear someone might hear the shot and be tempted to investigate. When his clothes dried and he was dressed again, he grubbed up some worms beneath a rotten log, cut a branch for a pole, and returned to the shallow lake. Within a few minutes he had a bite. He was jubilant as he swung the thrashing bass up onto the bank. It was nearly two pounds and the first fish he had caught in years, since he and his father had gone fishing when Rankin was still in high school.

He looked at the fish, its dark and silver scales gleaming in the sun. It was big enough for two or three meals. Maybe he could survive by living off the land after all. He had been discouraged by his efforts to catch fish on the island. He did not like to think about the island.

That evening he finished the rest of the fish he had not eaten for lunch, then drifted down to the edge of the swamp. In the twilight the swamp's bleakness seemed almost beautiful now. And, so far, it had proven a good hideout. Karen had chosen well. Thinking about her gave him a sudden melancholy twinge. He realized he missed her, and he realized the absurdity of allowing himself to miss her. He grew angry at his thoughts. Even though this place had been temporarily safe, he could not stay here indefinitely. Sooner or later somebody was bound to come around and discover him. In a few more days he would be strong enough to travel again, and then he would leave. But leave for where?

As he stood there mulling over these thoughts, from the corner of his eye he caught a movement in the weeds a few feet away. The tops swayed and as he turned, the weeds divided.

A giant cottonmouth slithered into view.

Rankin jumped back, nearly lost his balance, and almost toppled into the swamp.

The snake's little yellow eyes glittered, its delicate forked tongue flicked out, and it hissed. Its brown and mottled body was thick as Rankin's leg and nearly six feet long. Its odor, like an old brass doorknob, was overpowering. They stared at each other, and Rankin jerked the rifle up to his shoulder. He wanted to shoot the snake, the ancient pariah, but something kept him from pulling the trigger. If it comes any closer, he thought, I'll kill it. The snake turned and flowed like dirty dishwater into the stagnant waters of the swamp. It was gone as quickly as it had appeared. Rankin felt his muscles that had been tensed to kill suddenly relax and a shudder passed through him. He could have run instead of raising the rifle and aiming at its tiny V-shaped skull. The urge to kill it had been almost instinctive or maybe he had simply wanted to kill it because he had the opportunity to do so; and, yet, at the last moment, he had stopped himself, and not because he had been afraid somebody would hear the sound of the shot. The snake had been afraid too, had not wanted trouble, probably only a meal, a frog or a rat.

Rankin felt strangely shaken. He turned away from the swamp and went back to the shack.

He sat a long time in the doorway of the shack, but she did not appear. She was not coming again; she would not run any more chances. She had already run too many as it was, and it was stupid for him to think she might show up again, stupid for him to think each shadow on the trail in the moonlight concealed her and that momentarily she would emerge from it.

At last, he rose and went inside. He ought to be glad, he told himself, she had the good sense to stay away, and part of him was; but another part of him felt disappointed and curiously bereft. He never should have opened up to her the other night.

He rolled himself up in the blankets on the floor. The smell of rotting wood was strong. Despite the mosquitos he would rather have slept outside on the ground, except for the memory of the cottonmouth. In his mind he could still see it slithering through the rank weeds. It took him a long time to fall asleep. When he did, he was in the Manchester railway station again with Wallace and Crews and Espinosa and the rest of his outfit.

Espinosa had his helmet off, a cigar clenched in his strong white teeth, and was trying to convince them they had time to go to a fancy restaurant for highballs and supper, then come back to the station and fight off the enemy who were advancing down the canal toward the heart of the city. Espinosa was laughing and he handed Rankin a note of permission from the Captain. Rankin reached for it and was lifted suddenly into the air. When the choking cloud of dust cleared, Espinosa's head lay against Rankin's stomach, but the rest of Espinosa was gone. Rankin rolled the head off him, the cigar fell from the strong white teeth into the trail of blood the head was leaving behind on Rankin. Overhead was gray sky where the station's roof had been. Nearby lay Wallace and Crews. By the twisted, unnatural positions they lay in, he knew they were dead. Screams, groans, shouts began to rise from the rubble. Rankin tried to rise, but his left leg gave way. Pain spurted up it like a flame. Then, despite the pain and blood, he was hopping madly on one leg out of the ruined, cavernous building and up the street, out-running medics who pursued him, until he was out of the city entirely and surrounded by green fields and emerald hills; and he was hopping up one of the hills because, on its top, stood Peg waving at him. But he could not reach the top, try as he might; he kept falling back down because of his hurt leg and, when he looked up, pleading with Peg to come down to him, she was gone. The hilltop was bare. Then he was in a gray hospital room and several doctors and nurses were probing his leg and talking about amputation.

He awoke bolt upright in a sitting position. Around him was the smell of rotting wood and, mixed with it, the faint scent of perfume.

"It's all right, " she said. She was sitting next to him. She reached out and touched his forehead that was damp with sweat.

"It must have been some nightmare. " She was very close.

"It was, " he said. He had had variations of it for years. Her hand had dropped to his cheek. He pressed it with his hand, turned his face, and stared at hers in the darkness. Outside the frogs yammered in the moonlight. Her face was still, her eyes on his were large and intent.

Then they were holding each other.

Their lips brushed for a moment, moved away, and he felt the warmth of her cheek against his, and smelled the clean scent of her hair. In a moment his mouth brushed hers again and he felt desire begin to stir him. She put her hands on his chest and pulled back slightly.

"I think you're feeling better. " Her voice was husky. "I brought you some more medicine. I thought you'd be running low. And a little food and a couple of books. And, oh yes, the Sheriff has given up looking for you. " She seemed breathless.

"Let's go outside, " he said. "I want to get out of here. "

They stood under the oak near the shack and he asked her how long she had been inside.

"Only a minute. You were tossing and muttering. At first, I thought you were awake. Then you suddenly sat up. I was afraid you might be delirious with fever again. What did you dream?"

He told her.

"Is that really how you hurt your leg?"

He nodded and told her about the rocket that brought the roof of the station down on them, severing Espinosa's head, and crushing Crews and Wallace, his best friends. His left leg had been pierced by a steel rod that had severed tendons and smashed his knee. It had taken almost a year for him to learn to walk again without crutches.

Since the war, he had never been able to talk to anyone about the train station and now, again, he had opened up to her. Maybe it was the moon or the frogs or the waking out of the nightmare to find her there that caused the words to flow. He did not know, except that he was able to talk to her like nobody else he had encountered since Peg. After he had finished, he felt self-conscious. He looked away from her toward the woods.

She took his hand. "Let's walk up to the spring. " She led the way up the trail.

"My cousins and I used to roam all over this place when we were kids, " she said. "There were some old grapevines near the spring we used to swing on. My uncle's farm was only a mile up the road. We used to have a lot of fun down here. That old shack was our hideout and, when it rained, we'd stay in it and eat peanut butter and jelly sandwiches and play like it was a fort and we were besieged. " She looked back at him and at the rifle he was carrying. "I never thought— " She did not finish.

"Does your uncle still have his farm?"

"No. After he died, my cousins sold it. One of them died in the war. The other one, the last I heard, lives in Houston and sells life insurance. The farm has fallen into ruin. The owner lives in town and the government won't let him plant anything. "

They reached the small, moss-covered clearing. The pool of water was silver in the moonlight. Karen knelt, cupped her hands to the water, and drank from her palms. Her hair hung down, half concealing her face from him. She wiped her mouth with her fingers and looked up at him, her eyes welled with moonlight drawing him to her.

"Still tastes as good as I remember, " she said.

Her breasts strained against the white blouse as she rocked back a little on her knees. He bent down, put his hands on her shoulders, and her moon-luminous eyes seemed to dilate. He sank to his knees and pulled her tight against him. Her mouth, cold from the spring water, gradually warmed. Their tongues explored.

They stretched out on the moss, their bodies strained against each other. His hands moved over her body.

When he started to unbutton her blouse, she stiffened a moment, then relaxed. She wore no bra. He cupped one of the firm breasts and between his fingers felt her nipple harden.

Kissing the hollow of her throat, he descended to the breasts, pale in the moonlight, drawing his tongue over the nipples, teasing them between lips and tongue. Her hand tightened on the nape of his neck.

With his tongue, he laved the hollow of her navel and felt the heat building in his own belly. Her hands drew his face up again. Beneath her half-closed lids gleamed a hunger, now like the one within him. They struggled out of their clothes, her long milky legs opened, and she grasped him. With a quick intake of breath, she guided him into her.

They locked into each other's rhythm and soon she started to moan. He looked at her. The two vertical lines between her eyebrows were contracted into a frown, her mouth was slightly open and her eyes closed, her hair spread out against the moss. She clutched him tighter, cried out, and then his own need took over; she blurred and he became like a blind man lost in only one sensation.

They uncoupled and lay on the moss holding hands, waiting for their breathing to become normal again. She turned to him with a throaty laugh, reached over, and traced his eyelid.

"I pronounce you completely well. In fact, if you get any better, you'd be outlawed. "

"I already am. "

They both laughed. He felt drained, not just physically but of the anxiety and fear that had been with him since the moment he came upon Ross. She began to lick the sweat off his chest.

"M-mm. Very salty. I need a drink. " She leaned over to the spring and drank on her belly, her lips to the water. He put a hand on her white buttocks; she wiggled lewdly, turned and grinned, then resumed drinking. He crawled over beside her and drank too. Suddenly cold water stung his face as she splashed him.

He rolled over on her and they wrestled, giggling like children until they tumbled into the icy water.

"Oh, you bastard, " she shrieked. "It's freezing!"

"It was hot a minute ago. "

She pounded his chest with a fist. "Let me out!"

They scrambled from the water and collapsed on the moss. Immediately she began to shiver. He saw the goose bumps on her breasts and kissed them, his tongue smoothing the puckered flesh.

"Warm me, " she said. "Warm all of me. "

He covered her body with his.

"That's better, " she whispered.

In the heat between them the goose bumps vanished. After a while she pushed him away. He lay on his side and looked at her, but she pulled him over on his back and mounted him. She sat straight up, shifted her hips back and forth, and gradually the friction kindled his desire again. She bent over him, her wet hair hanging in his face but, when he tried to kiss her, her eyes glittered, and she shook her head whipping him with the damp strands until he clamped her face between both hands. She reached and brought him into her, arched back up to her sitting position. In the moonlight he watched her slowly rock back and forth, watched her eyes begin to glaze. He let her set the pace, and when the intensity began to build, she bent forward, her breasts flattening against his chest, her mouth finding his. He gripped her buttocks. The cold had vanished. Sweat covered them in a slick film. They built slowly to such a level of intensity that afterward they looked at each other in wonder.

Feeling boneless, he gazed up at the stars.

At last she broke the stillness. "Rankin, " she murmured. "Tom Rankin. "

"What? "

"I just wanted to say your name. "

"As long as you don't do it in public. "

Finally they dressed, drank from the spring and started back down the trail.

"I always liked that place, " she said. "Now I know why."

But as they neared the shack, reality began to take over again. She would leave in a few minutes, and he did not want her to go. Yet she had to, he recognized that. There could be no possible future for the two of them together. She had given herself to him this time for whatever reason; he was not sure she even knew—pity, desire, gratitude for saving her son, all of these or none? Did it even matter? For a brief time she had allowed him to lose himself with an intensity he had never experienced even with Peg.

And, she had run a grave risk in doing it. He should be and was grateful. But she could not continue running such risks and, from her silence, he guessed she was thinking similar thoughts.

"I want to ask you something, " he said. "Right before you drove me down here that day, you said something like 'I'm not going to let it happen again and do nothing. Not again!' What did you mean?"

She looked at him, then away, and said nothing.

"Listen, when you told me the Sheriff was coming, you were scared. You wanted me away from your trailer and I don't blame you. You didn't want anything more to do with me, and I don't blame you there either. What caused you to suddenly change your mind and bring me down here? That's all I want to know. "

She was stony-faced. Although the moonlight made her face pallid, it seemed to have suddenly become even paler. They had reached the shack now, but she did not stop. She kept walking toward the rutted trail and her car. He held her arm and pulled her around to him.

"Let me go, " she said. "I've got to go. "

Her eyes were bleak as the swamp.

He put his arms around her and held her. "Tell me, please. "

After he released her, she was still silent.

"All right, " he said. "I'll walk you to the car. "

Halfway to the car, she stopped and turned to him. She began to talk slowly, haltingly. Her husband was working late one night and her son was in bed, when she heard someone knocking at her back door, she said. At first she was afraid, because they lived on the edge of town; it was getting late, and there were no neighbors who lived behind them. She switched on the back light and saw him.

"I didn't recognize him for a moment, " she said. "In only a week he had changed so much. He looked so frail as though he had aged twenty years and was an old man suddenly. Then I saw he was bleeding. 'Help me, ' he begged, 'and for God's sake, turn off the light. ' I still had the screen door locked between us. We had known him for over a year. He was a lawyer, and we had had them over to dinner and they us. A week earlier, someone had informed on him. They had found a small printing press in his attic. He was publishing a small underground newspaper, they said, calling for the overthrow of the government. Chuck and I had been shocked. We had known nothing about it, never had a single hint. He had escaped just before they broke in, and we thought he had left the city. Now, suddenly, here he was at my back door begging me to hide him. People were after him, he said. They were closing in, and he could not run any more; he was too weak. 'Open the door, ' he begged me. 'Please, hide me. ' " Tears welled up in her eyes. "I told him to go away. I'll never forget the look in his eyes. I closed the back door and locked it. Then I stood there with my back against it. In a little while I heard the sound of voices. I prayed to God he was gone. "

Tears ran down her cheeks, but it was a silent crying. Then she stopped.

"They caught up with him and killed him a little while afterward. I didn't find that out until the late news. First, I called Chuck and told him to come home. He said he couldn't right then, and I couldn't tell him why I wanted him to on the phone—they're all tapped; so I told him Jeff had gotten suddenly ill. When he got home and I told him, he said I had done right and that Arthur, the lawyer, was a stupid fool. I wanted Chuck to hold me; I wanted to tell him how awful—how awful I felt for what I had done, but he was praising me for it. Then the news came on the wallscreen. He had been killed by some teenagers in a field less than a quarter of a mile from us. They had beaten him to death. Two of them had evidently come across him hiding in a house being built a couple of blocks from us. He had fought with them, gotten away, and come to me; by then the teenagers had gotten some friends and were hunting the neighborhood for him. They found him all right and split the reward money. " She looked away at the trees, but he knew she was not seeing them.

"All night Chuck kept telling me I had done the right thing— and he meant it. I realized, then, that I had never really known him—and that he didn't know me. We never have mentioned it since that night—not once. It happened four years ago, and we've never talked about it. I've never told anyone else about it—until now. "

He wanted to say something to her, but he realized there was nothing he could say that would help.

"Well, " she said at last, "Dad will be wondering where I am. "

He held her a moment. It was all he could do.

CHAPTER SIXTEEN

In the morning he took a long walk. He wanted to sort out some things, but mainly he wanted to walk until he almost dropped, because he was still keyed up from being with her last night. After she had left, he had been unable to sleep for thinking about her and about her story.

For four years she had been carrying a heavy load of guilt. Maybe she had entered the "subversive" picture by her student in the art contest to partly atone for what she felt was her cowardice that night in turning away her fugitive friend. The memory of that night had caused at least part of the rift between Karen and her husband. And, now he understood why she had helped him, brought the food and medicine, taken the chances she had—not just because he had saved Jeff, her son, but because of guilt. Had she given herself last night out of guilt too? At least, she had told him. Maybe having talked about it would bring her some kind of relief. The idea that she made love with him at the spring simply from guilt was ridiculous, he told himself. Yet it continued to torment him. Why? Then he knew the answer. He was falling in love with her. It was absurd, worse than absurd, it was hopeless—an enemy-of-the-state running from everyone had no right to fall in love, to subject anyone he cared about to his own danger. He knew that and yet it did not help.

For a few minutes he thought about not going back to the shack at all. But, he told himself, he was not quite strong enough yet to push on to the coast or wherever he might be headed, since he was no longer sure of that either. Finally, he decided he would return to the shack only for another day or so. By then he would be more ready to travel. Even so, the real reason he was going to stay a little longer was the hope that he might see her one more time.

He cursed himself for his own weakness.

When he got back to the shack, he still could not sleep. He stared at the rotting walls and the vines snaking in through the broken panes of the windows. His glance fell on the sack she had brought last night. He picked it up and emptied its contents on the blankets—another cake of soap, a toothbrush and a tube of toothpaste, a couple of tomatoes, a tin of beef stew, another vial of the same pills he had been taking, a loaf of bread, and two old paperback books. He looked at the titles: *One Day in the Life of Ivan Denisovitch* and *Stories of Anton Chekhov.* He had never read anything by either author; he only knew they were Russian and, therefore, the books were prohibited.

He checked the dates of publication and found both were printed long before the war. Karen must have hidden the books instead of turning them in as the law required. Bored and restless, he began reading the table of contents in the Chekhov book. One title caught his attention and he turned the fly-specked, brittle pages to the story, "In Exile. " He read it with mounting excitement in fifteen minutes. He read the next story called simply "Grief, " about a man who had lost his only son and wound up pouring out his heart to his horse, because no human being cared. It was as though the author had reached out from the pages of both stories and grabbed Rankin by the throat. Whoever this Chekhov was, he knew loneliness and pain all right and made you feel it.

Rankin wondered if Chekhov had ever been in exile, since he described the feelings of aloneness and misery so powerfully, authentically. At the end of the book was a brief biographical note saying he had written some plays, as well as stories, and that he had died in 1904, but no mention of his ever having been in exile in Siberia where the story had taken place.

By evening, he had read most of the stories in the book. He wished he had known Chekhov, wished the man were here in front of him now so they could talk. The man had understood what was important in the human heart. What difference did it make that he had been a Russian? That such a book should be banned and kept from people made Rankin angry. He had never thought that much about books before—he had read sometimes when he was bored with television—but now he understood, for the first time, why some people had been so upset during the great book burnings during the war and afterward.

Inside the shack the light had begun to fade. He rose and went to a window. The swamp water had turned blood-like in the setting sun. He gazed out at the desolate swamp. He remembered from the history books that Russia had been a police state under Czars long before it was Communist. Yet, it had produced a writer like Chekhov. He wondered if Chekhov had fled Russia or been punished by the authorities for a story like "In Exile."

Rankin went back and picked up the other book by the other Russian. It was yellowed with age and half-falling apart. According to the biographical sketch, Solzhenitsyn had been sent to a forced labor camp in Siberia as a political prisoner, yet had written the book based on his own experiences in the camp while still living in the Soviet Union, but later had been forced to leave his country by the Communist government. Rankin decided to read the book tomorrow. At least, the government had not put a price on Solzhenitsyn's head, but the man must have defied the government to write a book so critical, according to the publisher's note, of the existing dictatorship while living within its reach. Solzhenitsyn had fought with his only weapon—words. And he had not run.

It was nearly dark, and he realized he was hungry. He had eaten nothing since the night before. He ate a tomato sandwich, then went for a walk along the edge of the swamp, keeping a careful watch for snakes. After an hour he returned to the shack. He was weary and he crawled into the blankets. He had not expected her to come, but he had hoped. He stil hoped she might appear later in the night as she had the night before.

She didn't.

Rankin looked up from the book in time to see a big bass arc out of the water, then disappear again, leaving hardly a ripple on the lake's surface. He had been fishing for several hours without success and reading the Solzhenitsyn book. It was short and he was almost finished. He wondered if Karen had known exactly what he would see in the book—that Ivan in his prison camp was not only like Rankin himself in his struggle for survival, but like most of the citizens in the country in some ways. True, most were not enemies of the state, but the state was like a vast prison camp with the military as guards, with rationed food, an elite few exempt from any restrictions who ran the camp, and for anyone who defied their rule, punishment and death.

Again, Rankin read the brief biographical note at the beginning of the book to make certain that the author had, indeed, actually written and published the book while still living in the Soviet Union with its vast repressive machinery to squeeze an individual into any shape it desired, any attitude. He was filled with admiration for this Solzhenitsyn, even more than for the book itself.

He stared out over the lake, but he did not really see it because, in his mind, he saw the emaciated school teacher, Sam Ross, before him again when the Sepo patrol car pulled up at the gate of the barge depot that night. Ross had done something Rankin had scoffed at and thought incredibly foolish in nailing up copies of the Bill of Rights, a defunct document out of another age. And, in the end, he had died for it, while giving Rankin a chance to escape.

But, now, he saw a certain similarity in what Ross had tried to do and what Solzhenitsyn had done—both had tried to use words to fight oppression. Rankin glanced down at the rifle beside him. Neither man, despite his courage, had really changed anything, Rankin thought. Maybe they should have tried bullets.

He picked up the rifle. And, for all the luck he was having with a pole and line, maybe he should try to shoot the fish.

He was bored and almost wished he would come across another cottonmouth. The swamp at dusk seemed incredibly dismal. In the city he was used to being alone, but not such solitude with only frogs and snakes for company. The only reason he had stayed here this long was the hope of seeing Karen one more time, but she had not come the previous two nights. He decided tomorrow he would be ready to travel. The ache in his chest and the cough had disappeared, and he only felt an occasional twinge in his shoulder. Tomorrow, then, he would leave.

But the thought of never seeing Karen again filled him with melancholy. He decided to go back to the lake and try a little night fishing. The bass were feeding and he caught two good sized ones within fifteen minutes of his arrival, then they quit and, after an hour, he did too.

He took the fish back to the shack, cleaned them, and cooked them over a small fire, ate a portion, and wrapped the rest in the sack Karen had brought the supplies in the night they had made love. He wished he could get his mind off her.

He went up to the spring and took a quick, cold bath.

A breeze cool enough to raise goose bumps had sprung up, and he dressed hurriedly and headed back to the shack. Leaves fluttered down from the nearby oak, and his heart jumped as a slender figure emerged from its shadows. The scent of her perfume reached him in the breeze. His heart pounded.

"I'm glad you came, " he said.

"I almost didn't. I can only stay a few minutes. "

He started to hold her but felt the tenseness in her and dropped his hands. Her eyes were on his but it was as though she were looking through him and beyond to some distant point.

"What is it?" he said. "What's wrong?"

She looked away. "The doctor didn't want to give me any more medicine. He wanted to know who was sick. He knew it wasn't Jeff or me—or my father. "

"What did you tell him?"

"That it was for a friend of mine. He didn't believe me. He gave it to me, but I could tell he didn't believe me. I can't go back to him any more. I can't get any more medicine from him. " She twisted her wedding ring.

"It doesn't matter, " he said, "about the medicine. "

A leaf fluttered down between them. She scuffed at it with her foot, then met his gaze.

"I'm afraid, " she said. "I'm afraid to see you any more— afraid for myself, afraid for Jeff. He's everything to me. " Her voice had risen, but now it became almost a whisper. "I don't regret the other night—any of it, but . . . "

Her eyes seemed a bit too bright even in the moonlight. She turned her face away.

He craved her like a drug addict craved opium. He wanted to hold her, to lose himself with her as they had the other night at the spring; yet each moment she was with him could be her last moment on earth and, by staying here as long as he had, he had been selfish beyond measure. The only excuse he had was that he loved her but, if you really loved someone, would you put her in such jeopardy, he thought. Even now she might have been followed, and he cast an involuntary glance up the rutted pathway where her car would be parked. He looked to see if she had caught it, but she was staring at the gnarled trunk of the oak.

It seemed bitterly ironic. In the seven years since the war he had never felt love for a woman, although he had slept with some. It was as if all those years he had been dead inside. Now, at last, this woman had come along, and he could not have her—ever, and here she stood within arm's reach, warm, passionate, lovely. He felt like pleading with her, begging her to stay for only an hour, a half-hour more.

But the words came out of him, and it was like someone else speaking: "You'd better go now."

She nodded. Moments passed, and they both stood motionless.

"I'm leaving tomorrow."

Her eyes suddenly focused on his again.

"Where will you go?"

He did not know, so he did not answer. He saw the two vertical lines between her brows deepen.

"It's better you don't know," he said.

She nodded again. She reached into the pocket of her jacket and pulled out a medicine vial. "Here."

He took it and felt the warmth of her hand for a moment. He wanted to hold her so much his hand trembled, but he stuck the vial in his pocket.

"My husband is coming in a couple of days to visit. He wants us back. Jeff misses his daddy a lot."

"Are you going back with him?"

"I don't know. I really don't. Maybe."

At that moment he felt sure she would, and sudden jealousy surged through him. He gazed out over the swamp at the dead trees pale in the moonlight. The whole scene looked unreal, like a vast studio set in an old movie.

"Promise me," she said, "that you will take your medicine. Please."

He turned back to her with a wooden smile. "Okay."

They were silent; then she started past him and suddenly they were holding each other close, her cheek warm against his. "Goodbye," she whispered.

"Goodbye."

He watched her walk away in the moonlight. She gave a small

wave over her shoulder but did not turn around. After she had disappeared, he still stood staring up the rutted trail.

A trace of her perfume lingered in the air like a ghostly presence.

He awoke shivering. It was still dark. A cold wind was blowing into the shack; leaves from the oak flitted like bats through the broken window and skittered across the floor. The memory of his leave-taking with Karen pierced him suddenly, almost with a physical pain. He lay for a long time beneath the blankets, cold but too listless to move. At last, he mustered up the energy to throw back the bankets and struggle to his feet.

Outside, gray was seeping into the sky over the swamp.

He rolled up the blankets, after putting his meager rations and the two paperback books inside, and tied them into a bedroll with fishing line; then, shouldering it and picking up the .22, he left the shack for the last time.

At the spring he knelt and drank, the icy water sliced like a knife down his gullet. The wind blew sharply against his face. He barely noticed. He thought of how she had looked lying naked on the moss in the moonlight reaching up to him.

He drank again, rose, and headed his way through the trees. He no longer had any real destination but, out of habit perhaps, he turned toward the south, even though one way seemed as good as another.

CHAPTER SEVENTEEN

As he trudged down the abandoned railroad tracks, the sun began to set. He felt the air growing colder, promising frost. He rounded a curve and crossed a rotting trestle over a sluggish creek. He debated on whether to spend the night under the trestle but decided to go on a bit further. The night before he had spent in a lonely country church next to a graveyard and had kept relatively warm. Now he hoped to find another four walls and roof before night and the cold settled in and he became too tired to go any further. He shivered in the chill twilight.

He came to what had once been an old gravel quarry. Red streaks lingered in the sky where the sun had set and were reflected in the yellow water at the bottom of the quarry. The far wall of the quarry had eroded into steep gullies and he saw perched on top of it an old unpainted shack with one side hanging over the bank suspended in air. Sooner or later, with enough erosion, the whole shack would topple into the quarry, but Rankin did not think it would happen tonight. He left the tracks, skirted around the edge of the quarry, and climbed up the eroding embankment to the shack.

It was dark and forlorn and, although rags and cardboard had been stuffed into holes in the shattered window panes, it had the look of a place long deserted. But he held the .22 ready as he pushed open the door. He tried the flashlight Karen had given him. But it no longer worked. The batteries must be dead, he thought.

Inside waiting for his eyes to adjust to the darkness, he smelled the man before he saw him—a smell of sweat, a long-unwashed body, and gin.

Rankin tensed and backed up against the wall, swinging the rifle barrel around the room as his eyes tried to pierce the gloom.

"No need for firearms, " said a voice to his left. "No need at all. "

Rankin whirled in the direction of the voice and saw the vague outline of a figure crouched against the wall, but he could not make out the features.

Rankin covered him with the rifle.

"I wish you would not point that at me. " The man belched. His words were slightly slurred. "Allow me to introduce myself. " He rose with some effort to his feet. "I am Jack Tyrone. " He held his hand out and advanced a couple of steps.

Rankin ignored the outstretched hand, but lowered the rifle. "You live here?"

The other lowered his hand and looked around. "In this hovel?" He sounded genuinely indignant. "Of course not. I merely intended to pass the night here. I only arrived shortly before you. As a matter of fact I saw you from the window, there, standing below on the tracks. Did you happen to bring something to eat?"

Rankin's first impulse was to leave. The man seemed drunk, but he might have recognized him, even though it was nearly dark and the tracks were a hundred yards away. But, if he did leave, he would have to tie the man up so he could not alert the authorities. And yet, he did not relish stepping back outside into the cold and sleeping in a ditch or the brush. He stepped over to the man and ordered him to turn around.

"What are you going to do? I assure you I have no money. "

Rankin searched him, including the heavy coat he wore, to make sure he had no weapons. Rankin envied him the coat. Despite its fragrance, he decided he might take it in the morning. It was old and shabby, yet better than nothing. In one of its pockets was a quart of gin. Rankin told him to turn back around. In addition to the coat he wore a greasy fedora. In the darkness his face was only a pale blur, his breath reeked with the sweetish smell of gin.

"Actually I can do without food, " Tyrone said, checking his pocket to make sure the bottle was still there. "I just thought if you happened to have some with you . . . myself, I hate dining alone. "

He pulled out the bottle and, removing the cap, took a

generous swallow and offered it to Rankin.

Rankin shook his head, and the man walked back to the wall and sat down. "Be careful of that end, " he gestured toward the other side of the shack. "The floor is rotten and you might fall through into the water. It would not do to take a bath on a night like this. " He chuckled. "No, indeed. "

Rankin wondered when was the last time Tyrone had taken a bath—probably not for months. He sat down near the door, a good distance from him. It was not much warmer in the shack than outside. He unrolled the blankets and wrapped himself in one. He still felt cold. It was, he reflected, going to be a long night.

"Sure you won't have a libation, " Tyrone said. "Nothing like it to warm the cockles of your heart on a cold, cheerless night. "

He might as well, Rankin thought. He got up, walked over, took the bottle, and tilted it to his lips. It burned down his throat and chest and made tears spring to his eyes. It had to be at least one hundred proof and made illegally since the bottle had no label.

He went back to his blankets and got the paper sack with the last portion of the fish he had caught two nights ago when he and Karen had parted.

He offered some to Tyrone.

The man ate greedily, sucked the bones, then his fingers.

"If I had known there would be fish, my dear fellow, I would have chosen a white wine, " he said. He contented himself with a slug of gin. He passed the bottle to Rankin who could barely see it by the starlight through the window. He took a drink and shuddered, but soon a warm glow began to spread in the pit of his stomach.

Tyrone struck a match and lit half a cigar. By the tiny flame Rankin made out a gray beard, an aquiline nose, and protuberant bloodshot eyes, observing him somewhat blearily for an instant before focusing on the tip of the cigar. He blew the match out and began to puff on the cigar. He offered Rankin a drag which he declined. Rankin guessed he was anywhere between fifty and sixty-five years old. He wished Tyrone would go back to his side of the shack, but the older man showed no inclination to do so. He spread his legs straight out before him. The tip of his cigar glowed brightly a moment.

"There is no good theater anymore, " Tyrone said abruptly. "It's deplorable. O'Neill, Williams, Beckett banned as decadent.

Of course, there is the bard, but all his tragedies are considered political and therefore suspect. You ever follow the theater?"

"No."

"Pity." The cigar glowed brightly again. "It used to be wonderful. No more. We still have comedies, but the intensity of tragedy is what I miss. Mere melodramatic pap is all you find nowadays. Worse than the cretinous stuff on TV. I used to be a theater critic, you know. But they closed my paper down."

"They closed a lot of papers down."

"True. But mine was a New York paper. Still, with what they've done to Broadway I suppose it's just as well. You never saw a Broadway show?"

Rankin shook his head. "This is a long way from Broadway."

In addition to being a lush and smelling bad, the old ruin was a liar, Rankin decided. But the man had betrayed no sign of having recognized him, and it was possible that, wandering around the countryside, he would not have seen Rankin's face on TV, or that he was simply too gin-soaked to know if he had.

"What did you do?" Tyrone said.

Rankin stared at him in the darkness. "What?"

"What did you do? I assume if you still were working you would not be spending the night in this." He gestured with the cigar's glowing tip at the dark space before them.

"I fish and hunt."

"Ah, that's why you carry the blunderbuss about with you, is it?"

"That—and protection."

"You feel you need protection?" He finished the cigar and stubbed it out.

"It's a dangerous world. You never know who can be trusted."

"True. But let me assure you . . ."

"Don't assure me of anything. Just go on back over to the other wall and don't move from over there until morning."

"You wound me, young man," sighed Tyrone and belched. He got unsteadily to his feet. "You don't suppose I could have that other blanket, do you? That is if you're not going to use it."

Why not let him have it, Rankin thought. He had already decided he would not sleep tonight, but simply rest and keep an eye on his companion. He handed the lighter blanket to Tyrone who wrapped himself in it like an Indian and retreated to the spot he had occupied when Rankin first entered the shack.

For a long time Tyrone was silent. Rankin began to wonder if he should tie him up but, while he was debating, he heard a loud snore. Soon the snoring became regular. Rankin relaxed. With as much gin as Tyrone had apparently consumed, he ought to sleep for hours.

Rankin made up his mind to leave well before dawn. By the time Tyrone awoke he would be a long way from the shack. He reached for the other blanket and found the gin bottle. He draped the blanket over him to ward off the increasing chill inside the shack and held up the bottle to the window. It still held a couple of generous swallows. He set it back down, and his thoughts drifted to Karen. He wondered what she was doing at that moment. She had said her husband was coming. Maybe she was with him now, maybe she was in bed with him. Even with the blanket he was still cold and his thoughts did not warm him at all. He reached for the bottle. Uncapping it, he took a slug and felt the sudden warmth flow from his throat into his belly.

Through the window the stars gleamed, lonely and incredibly distant.

Tyrone's snoring rasped in his ears. Rankin finished the gin.

He awoke and, at first, had no idea where he was. Then he saw the window and a few stars and remembered. He had been more tired than he had thought to drift off as he had. His shoulder ached with the cold, his head throbbed slightly, the room was still. No snoring, no sound of breathing from Tyrone's side.

Rankin sprang up with the rifle. His eyes strained in the darkness. Then he saw the open window. With a sinking sensation in the pit of his stomach he saw it all. The old bum had feigned both drunkenness and sleep while purposely leaving the gin bottle within Rankin's easy reach, and he had fallen for it all—been outwitted by a sodden derelict. How long had he been gone? Why, why didn't I tie him up, Rankin thought. My God, why?

He rushed to the window. What he saw froze his blood and he nearly dropped the rifle. Three shadowy figures were moving toward the shack. He ran to the other window near the door. Several more figures were advancing toward him. There was no chance of escape out the door. He raised the rifle to his shoulder, then suddenly remembered that there might be one other way out. He crossed to the far side of the room and dropped to his hands and knees. The boards sagged beneath his weight. They were soft—as Tyrone had said—with rot. He reached down into a large space between two planks and peeled off a huge chunk of wood flooring like bark. Through the hole he saw a patch of water with stars glimmering on it. He was on the side of the shack that overhung the embankment. In a few seconds his nails were broken and his fingers began to bleed, but the hole grew. He clawed up wood feverishly. Outside a footstep sounded near the door. His throat tightened but he kept digging at the wood and suddenly the hole seemed just big enough. He stuck his legs through it, grabbed the rifle and, as he dropped through the floor, the door crashed open.

He landed on hard clay and slid into icy water that snatched his breath away. The water closed over his head and when he came up, the rifle was gone—it lay somewhere in the muck at the bottom. Above him were voices; he ducked under the water and began to swim, ignoring the stab of pain in his shoulder.

This time when he surfaced, he saw a cone of light shining down onto the water from the hole in the floor. Already he was numb, and he kicked toward the gully bank. He dragged himself up out of the water and began to climb the steep incline. A voice yelled from the shack and somebody replied from the railroad tracks across the water.

From the direction of the tracks came a dull whooshing sound. His wet clothes weighed him down, his teeth chattered, and he could barely hang onto the hard clay, but he kept climbing. The top of the embankment drew closer.

Suddenly it was like daylight. Frost glistened inches from his eyes on the gully bank, while above him the flare seemed to hang forever. Next to his left hand the earth burst away in a huge chunk and stung his face. With his right hand he reached up and grasped a clump of frozen weeds and hauled himself over the gully's rim. Below, the rifle's report echoed and re-echoed off the quarry walls.

The flare died, engulfing him in darkness again. He got to his feet and ran away from the shack toward a wall of scrub pines. As he hobbled into the trees, another flare exploded above him like a giant flashbulb, sucking away the darkness. The eerie phosphorescent light seemed to turn the trees' shadows pale. His breath was ragged in his throat. Behind him he heard cries, but he could not tell how close they were. His cheek still stung from the impact of the frozen dirt, and he was shaking violently with cold.

He ran blindly, zig-zagging through the pines until he no longer heard any noise behind him, only the labored panting from his lungs that, despite the cold, seemed on fire. Tyrone must have found a town nearby to raise that many people. He must have recognized me from the start, Rankin thought. But never once had he given any sign—cunning bastard. They had shared food and the bottle.

Even now his head still throbbed from the rotgut gin. He stopped running. He had to think. He had left everything back there, the blankets, the books Karen had given him, the rifle— everything except the hunting knife in his belt, and a few pills left in the medicine vial in his pocket. If the pneumonia did not come back, it was not because he wasn't trying, but the men behind him were his immediate concern. They might have to wait until morning, but they would comb every inch of these woods. Still, first they would try to raise enough manpower to surround him. He would be caught in a noose if he did not move quickly. He must get far away from the search area before daylight and the only way to do that was to find a car. But where? Somewhere close there must be houses or a town.

He had no idea in what direction to go, so he decided to continue straight ahead. He forced himself into a trot. He had to keep moving or, with his wet clothes, he would freeze to death before sun-up.

He lunged forward and soon settled into a steady lope. Now and again he had to pause for breath and listened for any sound behind him, but if they were on his trail they were well back. The trees vanished and he was running across an open field, then he was in woods again. His lungs burned; he began to feel like he could not run more than the next step; after each step he told himself one more, then one more after that. Run, run, run, you bastard, run. The chant in his head seemed to keep time with his harsh breathing. Run, run, run! The woods ran out before he did and, beyond, scattered lights glimmered at him.

For an instant, he thought they were the lights of a search party; then he saw beyond them burned a few street lamps. Houses meant cars. The frozen field was barren of cover except for a big tree, three-quarters of the way across, but in the darkness he did not think anyone in the houses would see him, even if they happened to be up and at a window.

Crouching low, he started toward the line of houses. Halfway across the field he froze. Behind him the whirring noise became faster, louder, and he spun around to see the helicopter, skimming above the trees he had just left, and coming right at him. Its searchlight was not on, and yet it was coming straight for him as though on a string. The pilot had night glasses. He could see Rankin as clearly as if it were daylight.

Rankin whirled and began to sprint toward the houses. Behind him the whump, whump of the rotors drowned out the thudding of his heart. The machine seemed to be almost on top of him. Above the loud whir a metallic voice sounded: "Don't move!"

Rankin kept running. Ahead of him rose a giant sycamore.

A streak of light shot past him, singeing his thigh, and disappeared into the ground.

Laser! It was a Sepo helicopter. He hurled himself to the ground and rolled behind the thick trunk of the tree. Like a huge, angry dragonfly the machine first veered away, then started to come around the tree. Rankin saw a light appear in one of the houses, then another. Soon the whole town would be awake. He estimated the nearest house was less than sixty yards away, and he broke for it.

Behind him the angry whirring sound of the rotors grew louder. He had almost reached the back yard of the house when another bolt of light stabbed the ground in front of him. He began to zig-zag and weave like a crazy drunk. Then he was pounding down a concrete driveway and out onto a street lined with thick trees.

He turned to see the helicopter appear over the rooftop, hover a moment, then rise to clear the trees. A window in the house opened, a man, open-mouthed, stuck his head out and peered up at the machine. He did not see Rankin. He was an average citizen, irate at being awakened in this unorthodox way and completely unaware of the reason. Rankin envied him.

He turned and began to flee beneath the cover of the trees down the street. Behind him the helicopter still hovered in the same spot. The pilot could see through the darkness, but not through the still heavy autumn foliage of the oaks and maples. The pilot switched on the searchlight at last, and began to sweep it up and down the street. Rankin jumped into a thick hedge and suddenly the helicopter was passing directly over him. The leaves on the hedge bent under the wind of the huge, spinning blades and dust whipped into Rankin's eyes making them tear. The searchlight beam darted past him without pausing and continued up the street over potholes and clogged gutters, taking the machine with it.

Rankin saw that he was in the front yard of an old house with peeling columns and a large sign that read: Powell's Funeral Home. Except for the light on the sign, the place was pitch dark. Staying close to the hedge, Rankin skirted around toward the back.

The garage door was wide open. Inside the garage was parked a baby-blue Cadillac hearse, so long its nose stuck out the doorway. He tried the driver's door and it opened without a sound. A low mirthless chuckle escaped his lips. He gazed at the back of the hearse and thought of the irony of taking refuge here. This is where they wanted him, but horizontal in the back.

He slid behind the wheel. A moment later the helicopter passed overhead, its searchlight swept over the hood and then disappeared. He bent under the dash and reached for the ignition wires. Somewhere in the distance came the wail of a siren.

The engine stuttered, then throbbed into life. The back of the house remained dark, the driveway clear. He knew he had to move now. Already they would probably be sealing off the roads leading out of town. The big hearse glided almost silently down the drive and onto the street. He expected someone to appear at the doorway of the funeral home or at a window, but he saw nobody, and the helicopter was not in sight either. Keeping the headlights off, he mashed down gently on the accelerator. The engine's purr grew deeper; trees and houses flowed by like dark ghosts.

As he approached an intersection, he began to brake, and a police car, blue lights flashing, shot by on the cross street. He still had not turned on the headlights, and he did not know if he had been seen. Then he heard the squeal of sudden brakes. It was too late to stop and try to turn the limousine around. He shoved down hard on the accelerator and sailed through the intersection and glimpsed the police car in the middle of a U-turn, less than fifty yards away.

He turned the hearse down the first side street he came to, then another one, and he was on a gravel road with few houses, and then they quickly petered out as the speedometer needle climbed past the sixty mark. The blue flashing lights in the rearview mirror were several hundred yards behind him when he topped a hill. At the bottom was a turn-off onto another gravel road; he let off on the gas and tapped the brakes twice, cut the wheel hard, and slid into the turn. The rear end started to fishtail, and he almost slid into the ditch, but he straightened it out and hit the gas hard again. Behind him he saw the blue lights flash by the turn-off and continue up the other road. He leaned back against the seat and relaxed a little.

Suddenly he became aware that he was wet and cold and fumbled around the dash until he found the heater switch. Soon warm air began to flow over him. He was still worried about the helicopter; yet the road he was on was narrow, and the trees with their overhanging limbs formed a kind of tunnel above him. But he might run out of this tunnel any minute. He began to slow down. The big engine hummed smoothly. It was, Rankin thought, the finest automobile he had ever driven, even if it was old, and the owners had kept it in almost perfect condition.

He decided to switch on the radio. As he began to reach for the control knob, he glanced in the rearview mirror and his heart nearly leaped into his throat.

Right behind him, its headlights off, loomed the black shape of an automobile.

Even as he watched, he saw the car swerve over to the left and begin to pull up beside him.

Rankin pushed the accelerator to the floor. The big engine throbbed and the trees on either side became more blurred. Out of the corner of his eye he glimpsed the low, bullet-shape of the other car inch up until it was almost abreast of him. He shot a glance at it. It held two men, and the passenger gestured with his hand for Rankin to pull over on the shoulder. Then, like a snake, the barrel of a gun slid out the car's window, pointed at him.

Rankin ducked. A blinding flash of light was followed by the roar of wind, and cold air stung his face. The trees were a solid black wall rushing past; his vision was blurred by sudden tears caused by the wind. Half of the top of the car was gone. Jagged shards projected from the remaining half like metal teeth. Through his tears Rankin saw the man either grin or grimace as he raised the laser to fire again.

Rankin cut the wheel sharply and the man's eyes bulged. Metal grated against metal; the other car swerved onto the shoulder and abruptly dropped back while Rankin clutched the steering wheel and fought to keep the hearse on the road. He looked back and saw the Sepo thrust the laser back out the window at him.

Grimly Rankin yanked the wheel to his left and heard grinding metal again. The smaller car veered onto the shoulder, caromed back into the hearse, sending Rankin onto the other shoulder; but he turned quickly back into the road and slammed once more in to the Sepo cruiser, saw it hit the shoulder again and fall behind him. As the driver tried to bring it back into the road, the cruiser's rear end began to slide on the loose gravel. In the rearview mirror Rankin saw the car spin and slam into a tree with a sickening sound of rending metal and shattering glass.

He kept going. His hands were cold and sweaty on the steering wheel. He glanced once more in the rearview mirror. They had struck the tree almost head-on with tremendous force. He doubted that anybody could have survived that kind of impact.

"Jesus, " he whispered. "Jesus Christ!"

He slowed the hearse down until he seemed to be crawling along at thirty-five or forty. Before they crashed, the Sepos had probably radioed that they were pursuing him. If he kept going straight, he might hit a roadblock. After a mile, he came to a dirt road and turned down it. He followed it for ten or fifteen minutes and it began to get even more narrow and rutted. He kept looking for another road to turn down, hopefully a better one, but there was none. He did not dare turn around and go back to the gravel road. More Sepos might be on it; for that matter, one of their cars might be behind him on the dirt road now. He glanced anxiously in the rearview mirror, but could not tell if anything was behind him. He still did not turn on his lights and had to drive even more slowly as the road got worse.

To the east the sky was becoming gray. He continued down the road another mile, and it narrowed to the width of a single car. Brush scraped the doors on both sides. At last he came to a wooden bridge with no railings, spanning a wide creek. He got out of the hearse and walked to the edge of the bridge. He stepped out on the bridge. Several planks were missing and it looked too rickety to hold the weight of the big hearse. At any rate he would not take the chance.

He got back into the Cadillac, backed it up a little, then turned off the road and onto the bank. He crashed through brittle weeds and dying undergrowth until trees blocked his way. Then he pointed the nose of the hearse toward the water, shoved it into neutral gear, and as it started rolling, leaped out.

He watched it slide down into the dark water and disappear.

Far away he heard the sound of a helicopter, but soon the sound died.

At least, he thought, now they can't spot the hearse from the air. He crossed the wooden bridge and, after a few yards, he left the road and headed into the woods.

CHAPTER EIGHTEEN

He could tell by the number of lights it was a large town. Crossing the fields at dusk he had seen the glow of the lights on the horizon for several miles. Now he sat on a rotting log in a small clump of trees and stared at the small houses a few hundred yards away that marked the edge of town. His gut ached and his belly rumbled with hunger. For three days he had found nothing to eat, but a few grubs.

After the frost the weather had warmed again, but now a chill hung in the air. If he were to survive, he would have to get food and warm clothing soon, and he needed a rifle. The town would have what he needed. For the past three days he had hidden in thickets and woods, while men searched for him on foot and by helicopter, and each day he grew weaker. When he first saw the glow of lights on the horizon, he had made up his mind that, despite the risk, he would go there before he lost all his strength and take what he had to have or else they could finish him in the attempt. But now, looking at the houses, he felt his palms growing sweaty and a cold sensation in the pit of his stomach. He struggled to control the fear. In the end his hunger decided him. He rose from the log and started toward the houses.

As he entered the unkempt back yard, a skinny rat darted out of the weeds startling him, then slunk under the house. Rankin slipped swiftly past a lighted window and glimpsed a tired-looking Negro woman at an old stove. A smell of cooking peas wafted into his nostrils for a moment. Then he was crossing a hard-packed dirt street.

The street, except for a few lights in windows, was dark and devoid of street lamps. A door slammed nearby, and he ducked behind a scraggly chinaberry tree. Two houses down, a man stood on a tiny front porch, stretched, took a deep breath of cold air, then went back inside. As far as Rankin could see up and down the street, the small, unpainted houses crowded against each other.

He needed to find an empty house far enough from any neighboring house that he could enter it without fear of being seen. He crossed through some more back yards and emerged onto another street, a little wider, but no better lit than the first, and the houses were even more tightly packed together. Hands in his pockets, he shuffled down the dark street until he came to a slightly wider gap between two houses. He ducked into the gap and emerged into more back yards, and almost ran into a clothesline. He noticed another one in the adjoining back yard from which some white garments hung. On closer inspection they turned out to be sheets and pillow cases, but in the next back yard he came to, hanging on the line was a dark object that proved to be a man's denim jacket, still slightly damp from the wash. He put it on anyway. He would have liked something warmer, but until he found it, the jacket would do.

The smell of the peas had made his belly rumble more loudly. He scrambled over a rotting wooden fence and stood on the lip of a drainage ditch. He decided to follow it, hoping it would lead into a less densely packed neighborhood. He was determined to get some food, no matter what the danger, even if it meant having to penetrate into the heart of the town.

He slid down into the ditch, and the air became damper and colder. He passed through a dank culvert under a street and almost slipped in the mud and slimy leaves. But soon the ditch became concrete, and chain-link fences rose on either side. Going up for a look, he saw the houses were brick now, although still packed together like sardines. He kept going and passed under another culvert, then another.

Nearby he heard a murmur of voices.

He could not make out what they were saying on the street above him. The voices sounded hushed, yet intent. Although he could not make out any of the words, there seemed to be a kind of suppressed excitement or urgency in their tones, a tenseness that made him instantly alert—and curious.

He climbed up to street level and peered cautiously over the rim of the culvert in the direction of the voices.

Three men stood fifty feet away along the edge of the street. They all faced in the same direction. Beyond them a man and woman were staring in the same direction also and, beyond them, under a street lamp, he could see another, elderly couple facing the same way.

Rankin turned his gaze in the direction they were looking—the same direction he was following in the drainage ditch, but he could see nothing unusual, only dark roofs and trees rising above them. Still they kept on staring.

What the hell did they expect to see—flying saucers, the Second Coming?

On the other side of the street from the rest of the people, he noticed a little girl standing on the curb. She alone was not staring in the same direction the rest were. Instead, she picked her nose and gazed at them in frank curiosity. The front door to the house behind her flew open, and a woman hurried outside. She grabbed the child by the arm and dragged her toward the house. Rankin watched them disappear inside. The way the woman had moved and her grim silence indicated she was either angry or frightened —but about what?

All of the people seemed to have an air of expectancy, of waiting for something. Whatever it was, he had his own concerns. He eased himself back down into the ditch and continued in the same direction, but more cautiously now, his nerves, if possible, on even finer edge.

But hunger goaded him forward.

At last he came to a wide street spanning the ditch. Once more he climbed to street level. Diagonally across from him was a big food store. It was the size of a warehouse and rose above the street like a concrete fortress. It had no windows and the doors were barred with steel. A police patrol car was parked alongside it and Rankin could see the two men inside the car, one apparently asleep, his head lolled back. All food stores were guarded day and night—even the small ones.

Rankin peered at the barred doors and imagined the rows and rows of canned foods inside—corned beef, spam, corn, stewed tomatoes, beans, peas, soups, stews, chili. He licked his lips and suppressed a kind of sob. He stared at the police car, and his eyes burned with hate and frustration. Perhaps he could divert them somehow. But he knew it was hopeless. Even if he sent them off on a wild goose chase, he could not break through the steel bars without a blow torch. And even with a torch, it would be hopeless. The food store was a vault, and it had more elaborate alarms than any bank and a camera system that would be linked directly to a monitor in the local police station. That was one way they controlled the food supply at its retail source, along with strict rationing and, if you were caught stealing a grape, they would put you away for a year at hard labor.

If you were rich or well-connected, the rationing was not so strict. For everybody else, it was either the black market, what you could grow yourself, or nothing.

He turned his gaze away from the store and noticed that on either side of it were trees and behind them were old houses. They were set fairly wide apart. By crossing to the other side of the street and following the ditch, he could get behind them for a better look to see if one might be empty. He groped his way through the stinking culvert to the other side and stayed in the ditch until he was sure he was well out of view from the patrol car before he climbed up again. Then he scrambled over the chain-link fence and crept through waist-high weeds until he had worked his way back toward the street again, but far from the ditch and the police car. He could see the backs of several of the houses, all of them had lights in the windows, but one. He moved toward it. It was a gaunt, two story frame house, separated from the houses on either side by tall, rank hedges. His heart began to beat faster. But maybe nobody lived there. Yet as he drew closer, he could make out curtains at some of the dark windows.

He crawled under a rusty wire fence into the back yard that was weedy and unkept. Two cedar trees blighted with white splotches framed the back of the house. He crept past them toward the back porch, and a dank smell of rot and woodsmoke filled his nostrils as he climbed the steps. Cupping his hands to his face, he peered in the window. After a while he could make out a stove and a refrigerator. He left the porch and circled the house to make sure there were no lights on in the front. There were none. The house lay utterly still. Somebody might be inside asleep even though it could not be much after 9:00, he guessed; but the gnawing hunger in his belly, despite that possibility, drove him around to the back porch again. The back door was locked. He pried off the window screen then waited a minute, his ears strained for any sound from within. He tried the old-fashioned tall window, and it too was locked.

Pulling off the denim jacket, he wrapped it around his fist and drove it through the pane. Shards of glass shattered on the floor. With pounding heart, he waited for a light to switch on or footsteps. The musty breath of the house came through the broken pane.

He reached in, unlocked the sash, raised the window, and climbed inside. It was colder in the room than outside, and a faint odor of cucumber mingled with woodsmoke and rot. He pulled the jacket back on and went immediately to the refrigerator. He eased open the door and his heart fell as he surveyed the pitiful contents by the interior bulb—a half-eaten cabbage and a lump of something wrapped in cellophane. He unwrapped it and found a gray blob of rancid meat. Hungry as he was, its odor almost made him gag and he thrust it back on the shelf and tried a drawer under the freezer compartment. He found two thin slices of processed cheese, and wolfed them down as he continued his search.

In the vegetable bin at the bottom he found a whole raw carrot and began chomping it. Then he turned his attention to the cabinets on the walls. There were some cracked cups, saucers, a few dishes and glasses. At last he found a carton of powdered milk, but that was all. Where in hell was the food? Anger surged through him. Whoever lived here must have hidden it. He would tear the place apart until he found it.

He heard a creaking sound. His breath caught.

Someone else was in the room, and he reached for the hunting knife. The light dazzled him. Blinking, he made out a figure in the doorway, but it took a few moments to recognize it as a woman.

She wore a threadbare, shapeless gown. Her thin white hair rose around her skull in a kind of halo, framing bones that seemed to jut outside her parchment-like skin. One eye was gone. He stared into the socket with a queer fascination mixed with terror. For an instant he was afraid he might glimpse her brain. He tore his gaze from the bare cavernous socket to the other eye that stared back at him with a looney glee.

She began to laugh. It was chilling. The sound bubbled out of her throat and echoed emptily in the cold room.

Rankin ran to the door, fumbled with the bolt, and hurled himself outside. Leaping off the porch, he ran toward the front of the house as fast as he could go. Behind him the old woman's crazy laughter seemed to follow him. Even after he reached the street and pounded blindly down it, he thought he could still hear her laughter. When he came to his senses, he still held the hunting knife. He put it back in its sheath and looked up and down the street to see if anybody had seen. The street was deserted.

He hurried down the street, uncertain as to the direction he was going, only anxious to put as much distance between himself and the old woman as possible. Whether it was the shock of her sudden appearance, the empty eye socket, or the fact that she was obviously insane, she had completely unnerved him.

She should have been in an asylum, not allowed to run around loose. Then he had another thought. She had been so thin, and he had taken from her pitiful food supply. Along with his anger and fear, he suddenly felt a hot flush of shame. He cursed and looked around him again. He had left the residential area and was surrounded now by dingy shops and offices.

Ahead, he saw the three gilded balls of a pawn shop, but beyond that he saw something else. An angry red glow rose above the roofs of the low buildings. As he stared, he thought he saw flames shoot up momentarily, then sink out of sight again.

He wondered what was burning. Whatever it was, it had to be a big fire to cast such a glow in the sky. He hurried on to the pawnshop. The window was covered with heavy steel wire, and inside it he could see watches, rings, a saxophone, a guitar, an expensive Japanese camera, and a double-barrelled twenty-gauge shotgun.

In the distance he heard sirens. They were moving toward him but down a different street. He continued to gaze at the shotgun. A couple of doors beyond the shop lay the entrance to an alley that might give access to the rear of the pawnshop, he thought. As he started toward the alley, he heard a sound like an angry muttering ahead of him.

From around a corner two blocks ahead appeared a man. He was running toward Rankin. A moment later two others appeared, then several more. Rankin darted into the alley and in a few yards was surrounded by darkness. But, after only a few more yards, he came to a solid brick wall. He realized he was trapped in a cul-de-sac. He could hear the sound of footsteps pounding on the pavement now and knew it was too late to go back to the street, and he was not sure if they had spotted him. He crouched against the cold, clammy bricks, drew the hunting knife and waited, eyes strained toward the street.

A shape sped past the alley, then another, and then a mass of shapes, and what he had first taken to be angry muttering now became groans, curses, and labored panting of men gasping for breath. A few more straggling shapes passed the alley and the sound of pounding feet receded.

Madness, he thought. First the old woman, now a conflagration and people fleeing from it instead of running toward it, while he crouched in a dank alley holding a knife—it seemed to him the whole world was mad as the sirens shrieked louder, and that he was in the vortex of the madness and there was no escape. Again he felt panic as he had in the presence of the old woman, and he had to get out of the alley.

He had almost reached the street when he heard more footsteps, but they were not running, but moving in a kind of fast shuffle, and it sounded like something was being dragged. He retreated back into the shadows.

"He's finished," a voice whispered. The speaker was breathing hard.

"You sure?" gasped another voice.

"Yeah. We got to leave him."

"Set him down in the alley here."

They came into the alley—two figures supporting a slumped third whose feet dragged the pavement. Rankin crouched low, knife at the ready. The two lay their companion down on the pavement. One of them bent over him a moment.

"You sure he's dead?" he said.

"Yes, yes. Let's get the hell out of here before they come."

"God!" the kneeling one said in a choked voice. "God damn!"

"I'm leaving." The other one cast a glance back in the direction of the fire. Then he was gone, fleeing after the others.

"Wait!" cried the man rising quickly from the inert figure. Then he was gone, too.

Rankin moved slowly toward the still body. The man had on an old Army field jacket. Rankin bent down and suppressing a tremor started to unbutton the jacket. He could not see the man's face. His face was turned away from the light and he wore a baseball cap and its bill covered the face in even more shadow. But as he rolled him over to tug the jacket off, the head lolled to one side, knocking the cap off and Rankin saw the face in profile, pale and boyish, not over fourteen or fifteen years old.

Then, he saw the scorched hole through the belly of the ragged plaid shirt. The Sepos had killed a mere boy. Gazing at the boy's face, Rankin suddenly felt a little sick. He looked away. Now the full significance of what he had seen earlier—the little groups of people standing on the street expectantly, the mother snatching the little girl up and dragging her into the house—slowly dawned on him. They had known what was going to happen or had at least suspected it. The fire, the fleeing people, and this boy with a laser hole put through him by Sepos meant there had been some kind of demonstration that had gotten out of hand, become a riot perhaps.

Yet to kill a boy—Rankin fought down the wave of nausea that rolled up from his belly. He straightened up, leaving the jacket, stared toward the fire that now seemed to be burning fiercely out of control. Flames spurted up over the roofs of the low-lying buildings casting an eerie light. Sirens screamed nearby. Except for the sound of the sirens he would have had the feeling that everything—the fire, the stampede of people, the dead boy—was unreal. But it was real; the laser hole through the boy's guts was real. Rankin stepped out of the alley and began to run. He headed in the direction the others had taken—away from the fire.

He had gone less than a block when he heard the car coming. He slunk into another alley. Behind him the car slowed and turned into the alley—its headlights threw Rankin's shadow far ahead of him. The alley opened into another street and he fled headlong down it until he came to a deeply recessed doorway and ducked into it. Behind him, stairs climbed into blackness. He raced up them, reached a landing, and below saw the car's lights flash past the doorway.

"They're all over the place. " The voice was almost in Rankin's ear and his blood froze.

"Were you down at the river?" the voice whispered.

Rankin's pulse hammered. "No. " He could see nothing in the darkness.

"Who are you then?"

A match suddenly flared. Less than two feet away cool eyes stared at him through rimless glasses.

"You can put the knife away, " the man said.

Rankin saw the glint of recognition in the other's eyes. Yet they continued to regard him coolly.

"I think you know me, " Rankin said. He put the point of

the blade against the man's throat.

"It would be hard not to. " The man spoke calmly, easily. His gaze did not flicker from Rankin. "You've been on television several times lately. Why don't you put the knife away?"

Rankin shook his head. The match went out.

"Do it!" snapped a voice behind him—a woman's. At the same time Rankin felt the cold metal of a gun barrel press into a spot right below his ear.

The man lit another match.

"Better do as Sheila says, Mr. Rankin. "

Rankin lowered the knife, and the man took it from him. The match went out leaving them in utter darkness again. But the gun barrel continued to press against his neck. Rankin waited for the woman to pull the trigger. Or maybe the man would use the knife instead.

The seconds dragged by endlessly. As Rankin waited in the darkness, his nerves began to unravel. The muscles between his shoulder blades began to jump. And he felt as though he wanted to pant. The cold pressure of the gun barrel bored into him.

"What the hell are you waiting for?" he said. "Get it over and be damned!"

CHAPTER NINETEEN

"Don't be stupid. " The man struck another match. He peered at Rankin over the flame with what seemed for a moment a hint of amusement in the cool eyes which had all the color of dirty ice. "Sheila would have killed you already if we wanted the reward money. "

"Then maybe she'll take the gun out of my neck. "

The man gave a quick nod, and Rankin felt the cold pressure of the gun barrel withdrawn from his neck.

"Frankly I'm surprised to see you here, Mr. Rankin. Didn't you know this town is crawling with troops and Sepos?"

"I got hungry. I still am. "

The match burned out and outside they could hear the scream of sirens heading toward the river.

"The fire must be spreading, " the man said. "With the wind off the river, it could burn down half the waterfront. " There seemed a kind of satisfaction in his tone. "You say you're hungry. After our friends out there settle down, we'll see about getting you some food. "

"Why?"

The man laughed without mirth. "Suspicious devil, aren't you?"

"What do you want?" Rankin asked.

"After we've had some supper we can discuss business. Sheila, check the street. "

"What about him, Paul?" The woman sounded dubious.

"If Mr. Rankin wants to go, he can. But he might prefer a meal first and at least listen to what we have to say. What about it Rankin?"

"Why don't you just say your piece now?"

"All right. Go on, Sheila."

The woman hesitated in the darkness, then her soft footsteps sounded on the stairs. Rankin saw her legs, then her hips descend into the dim rectangle of the doorway.

"There was trouble down at the river tonight," the man said softly. "It began as a peaceful demonstration for more food. A fully loaded grain barge sprang a leak last night and the towboat shoved it ashore here. This morning troops began transferring the grain to another barge. Needless to say, the grain was not for us, but word got around and all during the day a crowd gathered to watch. By dark we had organized a rather large demonstration complete with signs demanding more food."

Below, the woman flattened herself against the wall and a car sped past the doorway and kept going.

"They brought in a squad of Sepos," Paul resumed, "and told us to disperse. We didn't. Then some fool started a fire in one of the warehouses. When the firemen came, some of the crowd blocked their way. We were ordered to make way and when we didn't move fast enough . . ." The man spoke in a flat voice, but underneath for the first time Rankin sensed barely suppressed emotion. "They killed several of us."

The woman returned. "I think if we hurry we can make it. They'll be combing the streets pretty soon, the bastards!"

"All right, let's go."

"I don't think I'm going anywhere," Rankin said.

"Suit yourself, then. Here." The man handed him something and then Rankin grasped the handle of his hunting knife again. "You're going to need it," Paul said. "Before long the Sepos will be doing a building to building search here—looking for wounded stragglers."

The man could be lying, but Rankin had a sudden vision of the dead boy in the alley. The man had not lied about the Sepos opening fire or the blazing warehouse. Undoubtedly he knew the town and the best escape routes and Rankin did not. Suddenly he made his decision. They had already reached the sidewalk when he caught up with them.

My luck, Rankin thought, to have picked the worst possible time to come scavenging here. What marvelous timing!

But he did not have long for such reflections. Already Paul and the woman were darting across the street into a space too narrow to be called an alley that ran between two dilapidated buildings. Rankin squeezed into the opening after them. Paul led them through a twisting maze of basements, back yards, and over fences. Then they were climbing over a stone wall and were in a wooded cemetery, a big one. Tombstones glimmered around them dully like decayed teeth, and once Rankin almost tripped over a freshly dug grave. The sound of the sirens could barely be heard now. They stuck close to the trees and passed a large vault that tunneled into a hill. After the sound of the cars and sirens, the stillness of this place seemed soothing, yet unsettling too. It was not the dead one needed to worry about, Rankin thought. It was the living, including the two just ahead of him, that were dangerous. And again he had the sensation that he was moving in some kind of dream—that he had dreamed of the crazy woman with the gaping eye socket, and the dead boy in the alley with the laser hole in his belly—that he was dreaming now that he was following two strangers through a graveyard toward God knew what place or what fate. He began to pant and not entirely from fatigue, although they had been moving at a fast clip for over a mile.

At last they came to the end of the tombstones, scaled another stone wall, and emerged onto an empty street and a neighborhood of one-story frame houses. There were few lights in any of the windows. They stayed in the shadows and hurried down several more streets of increasingly modest houses. Paul waved them back behind a dense hedge, then went on alone down a dark street. Rankin turned to the woman who crouched silently beside him. She took no notice of him; she was staring intently down the street in the direction the man had gone.

Rankin had almost decided to slip away when the man returned. "It's all right. Come on!"

He disappeared again into the darkness.

"I'll pass, " Rankin said and turned back in the direction of the graveyard.

"Just hold on, " the woman said. "Paul wants to talk to you. "

"No thanks. "

"Listen to what he has to say. " She grabbed his arm.

He pulled away from her, she reached into her big leather shoulder bag and suddenly was holding the gun on him again, a snub-nosed .38. Her eyes glittered. "I don't want to use this. But I swear I'll shoot you if you don't do as I say. " Something in her eyes and tone left him with no doubt she would do exactly what she said. He heard the hammer click back on the revolver.

She directed him down the street after Paul, while staying well behind him. They stopped in front of a small, dark frame house and she motioned him toward the front door. As they reached the door, it swung open onto a dark little hallway and Rankin entered. Then the door shut behind him. Paul led them into another room.

"I thought I was free to go," Rankin said sardonically.

"Shut up!" the woman said. "He was going to run," she said to Paul.

"Put the gun away, Sheila. Hear me out, Rankin. Then you will be free to go or stay. I promise." He switched on a table lamp.

The room was not much bigger than the hallway; the shades at the windows were drawn tight. A beat-up sofa with a flowered pattern on the upholstery, a couple of worn easy chairs, a scratched coffee table, and a small television set filled the room, leaving them little space to stand.

Paul motioned Rankin into one of the chairs.

Reluctantly he sat in it. The seat sagged, but it was surprisingly comfortable. How long had it been since he had sat in any chair? Three or four weeks? He could not remember exactly. The days he had been on the run seemed to blur together. How long had it been since he had parted from Karen? Only five days—it seemed like months.

He looked at the woman. She was small with long brown hair hanging down to her shoulder blades. She shrugged out of her shabby coat, and he saw that she had surprisingly full hips and buttocks that stretched her faded jeans almost to the bursting point. She had a sullen, sensual mouth. She felt his eyes and her large brown eyes regarded him for a moment indifferently, then she went back into the hallway and hung the coat up in a closet.

When she returned, Paul asked her to go into the kitchen and fix some supper. She went without a word. Paul sat down across from Rankin in the other chair, and eyed him through the rimless glasses as the noise of clattering pans came from the kitchen.

Rankin leaned back in the chair and waited for the other to speak. They were, he thought, like two tomcats sizing each other up. Thin and wiry, Paul's head seemed a little large for his body giving him an almost frail appearance, but the cool, shrewd eyes held the quiet authority and decisiveness of a surgeon or a military commander.

"I hope you like bean soup. "

Although he was nearly starving, Rankin felt like a stiff drink and said so.

Paul shrugged apologetically. "I'm afraid I don't drink. In my business it can be a disadvantage. "

"What is your business?"

The other smiled. "Let's say I'm an organizer. "

"I see. Did you organize the protest at the river tonight?"

"I and a couple of others. "

Rankin looked at the worn carpet—a septic tank brown. Then he looked back at Paul. "People got killed. "

Behind the glasses the eyes took on a hard glint. "Yes. Some idiot started a fire—that was not part of the plan. " He steepled the fingers of both hands in front of him. "But this is war, Mr. Rankin, and there are going to be casualties. You don't think they are going to give up their power voluntarily?" His eyes bored into Rankin's.

"No, I don't think that, " Rankin replied mildly. "I also don't think a bunch of demonstrators are any match for laser guns and the U.S. Army. "

"If we were only an isolated group, I would agree. But all over the country people are fed up with things as they are—wide-spread hunger and rigid control. They are ripe to revolt. "

So that was his game—revolution. Now he understood why they had not killed him, and he knew what would be coming next. A ghost of a smile reached Rankin's lips. But first they would feed him and try to soften him up. Who knows, they might even offer him sex with the woman as a bonus.

Paul either caught the smile or read his thoughts and his tone grew cold.

"You think this is some sort of play-acting or pipe dream? This demonstration tonight was not the first—nor will it be the last,
I assure you.

Six weeks ago in Chicago there was a mass demonstration that made the one tonight seem penny-ante. Two weeks ago in Beaumont, Texas there was a massive food riot. "

Rankin wondered how many people were killed there. "How do you know this? They'd never print or broadcast news like that. "

"We have our sources—and, believe me, they are reliable. We are not alone here. We're linked up with other groups all over the country. "

Rankin suddenly felt very tired. He shook his head. "It's all happened before, " he said wearily. "Right after the war. People were killed or put in concentration camps and that was the end of it. "

"Yes. But that's because people and groups were isolated. Their demonstrations and riots were not properly organized. They happened spontaneously. There was no proper leadership or national coordination. This time there will be. Can you imagine what will happen when millions of us take to the streets at the same time all over the country? How could they stop us?" His eyes were no longer cool, but seemed to burn. "How can they stop us?" he repeated.

"With lasers. Like tonight. "

"It was too one-sided tonight. They had all the advantage. Soon we will go on the offensive and fight. "

"You still won't be any match for them. "

"We won't fight them in the open. Of course, they would cut us down. After we soften them up, then we'll go back to mass demonstrations. "

"How exactly, " Rankin asked, "do you plan to soften them up?"

"Through attrition. Each city will have specifically trained people—urban commandos. They will ambush troops, burn barracks and police headquarters, eliminate senior officials. "

"Terror tactics. "

"You fight fire with fire. You ever study any revolutions, Rankin? Look, you've already guessed why you're here. " Paul leaned forward in his chair. "We're organizing a freedom squad now. I want you to join us. "

Even before the bean soup, Rankin thought. He looked evenly at the other man.

"Freedom squads. They do the killing, right?"

"I told you we are in a war. " Paul's voice was calm again, only his eyes blazed with a kind of pale light behind the rimless glasses.

"I thought you would certainly understand the need for force, " the woman spoke from the doorway to the kitchen. "You killed two Sepos the other night. "

Rankin turned to her. So they were dead. He had thought so at the time, but until now he had not known for certain. In his mind he had seen over and over the car smashing into the tree with a sort of terrible clarity. He had had no choice—then. He gazed bleakly at her for several heartbeats, then turned back to Paul. The silence in the room seemed overwhelming.

"I don't think I'd make a good triggerman. "

"The revolution needs people like you. I'm offering you something to fight for besides yourself. Out there you're a hunted animal trying to survive from one moment to the next with no cause but your own survival. You could be part of us and help free the people. They want to be free—they want a better society!"

Rankin smiled wolfishly. "A better society! Free the people! That's good. Let me tell you about people. Those people you say want a better society, who want freedom—those people have hunted me for money. They've come after me with guns, ice picks, baseball bats—anything they could lay their hands on. And, if they didn't have the guts to do it themselves, they couldn't wait to inform. I saw an old lady put the finger on a man who was burned in front of my eyes. And I've got a nice, ugly hole in my shoulder from these same people who want to be free. You want to see it? They're free now to shoot at me, and let me tell you something—they like it. That's the kind of freedom they can understand. So talk to me some more about helping free the people. I can't wait to join your revolution. The only thing I worry about is who will shoot me first—the Sepos or the people I'm supposed to be fighting for. " Rankin stood up abruptly. "I guess this means I won't be eating any bean soup. " He started for the door.

"That's about what I expected, " the woman moved in front of him. Her neck muscles were corded. She blocked the entrance to the hallway, her body rigid and her legs planted solidly. "Don't you know why they've hunted you and others much better than you?" Her tone was angry and contemptuous.

"Greed, " he said. "Or blood lust or both. Get out of my way. "

"A few of them, yes. But most of them aren't that way. The government has used hunger and fear to turn us against each other. Divide and conquer. And they've done a great job with you. Look at you! Concerned only about your own precious skin. We're offering you a chance to unite with us and fight the real enemy, but you don't care to help anybody but yourself. You're selfish and stupid!"

"That's a nice little speech. Now get out of my way. "

They stared at each other and an almost electric tension seemed to vibrate between them.

"I think we are ready for supper, " Paul rose from the chair and laid a hand on Rankin's shoulder.

"Forget it, " Rankin said.

"No. I promised you supper and you shall have it. It's getting cold out there and some hot soup will do you good. Eat with us—please. " He smiled. "No strings. Honestly. " The aroma of the bean soup from the kitchen smelled delicious.

Rankin looked back at the woman whose face was now impassive again. She stepped past them toward the kitchen. "It's all ready. Both of you go wash your hands. "

Paul took Rankin's arm and led him into the hallway to the bathroom sink.

"You'll have to forgive us. Sheila and I are both very committed to the cause and we sometimes tend to forget not everyone sees things the same as we do. "

In the kitchen they sat down to a small table with one leg shorter than the others, so when you put your weight on it, it rocked and made waves in the soup. Rankin had to admit the soup tasted better than any he had ever eaten. It surprised him. He had figured at best that a revolutionary would be an indifferent cook, devoting most of her or his energy to less domestic pursuits. But then, he reflected, she could probably have fed him boiled urine and he would have thought it tasty. Her words had stung him and he kept turning them over in his mind while studiously avoiding even a glance in her direction. He had to acknowledge the truth of some of what she had said; yet something about them both bothered him. Maybe it was their very zealousness he mistrusted or maybe it was something else.

Rankin looked around the messy kitchen with its drawn shades and bolted back door, and his gaze finally settled on Paul.

"What do you do?" he said. "Besides being an 'organizer. ' "

Paul smiled. "You mean how do I pay, " he gestured at the room, "for all this, and bean soup too?"

Rankin nodded.

"I'm a chemist. I make artificial shit. " He set his spoon down. "I cook up vats of it to make our crops grow faster, so we can export them overseas quicker, so we can get the minerals and fuels for another war that nobody can win. How's that for logic? Meanwhile, Americans go hungry. " He picked up his spoon and resumed eating his soup.

Rankin looked at Sheila's left hand. There was no wedding ring.

As if reading his thoughts, Shelia gave him a slight, mocking smile.

"I'm a hooker—an ex-hooker. " She looked at Paul warmly. "He took me off the streets. " When she looked back at Rankin, her eyes had lost their warmth. "Does that answer your question?"

Before Rankin could reply, a knock sounded on the back door. All three of them froze.

Paul got up and silently beckoned Rankin. They went into the living room, then into the hall and Paul shoved him into the closet behind some coats and jackets and shut the door. He heard Paul's footsteps retreating back toward the kitchen. In the blackness he smelled the mustiness of the clothes. Then he heard the back door open. His hand rested on the knife handle and sweat trickled down his ribs. Footsteps approached; he pulled out the knife.

The closet door opened.

"It's all right, " Paul said. "Come on out. "

Rankin blinked at him and still clutched the knife.

"It's my niece. My sister sent her over to make sure we were all right. She didn't know whether we were among the casualties tonight. Come on and finish your soup. "

In the kitchen Rankin found a pale-faced girl with red hair and barely budding breasts. She stared at him owlishly for several moments.

Shelia brought her a bowl of soup and she sat down at the table and attacked it ravenously.

"Tell your mother I'll be over tomorrow, " Paul said. "Any word from your father?"

The girl shook her head and continued eating the soup. Rankin wondered if she might be a mute. After she finished the soup, she gave Rankin another wide-eyed look then slipped out the door into the darkness without uttering a word.

"Her father, a good man, is in prison, " Paul said bitterly, while Shelia removed the bowls from the table. "He stole a case of black-eyed peas from a delivery van because he had been out of work for six months. They gave him five years. That's the kind of government we live under. We haven't even heard from him in months. We can't even be sure he's still alive. "

Sheila came over and put a hand on his shoulder. Paul reached back and put his hand over hers.

"The only way we can bring them down, Rankin, " Paul said, "is to stand together and fight them like I told you. " Behind the rimless glasses the pale eyes bored into Rankin. "You can see that, can't you?"

"We're offering you hope, " Sheila said. "What have you got now?"

Maybe she was right. Maybe she and Paul did offer him his best hope—his only hope. Yet the dead face of the boy in the alley seemed to rise in front of him. Paul and Sheila were physically unharmed, but a boy lay dead. In any war there were bound to be casualties, Paul had said. But there had to be a particular kind of ruthlessness in a movement that would sacrifice the lives of kids. If the people before him were willing to sacrifice that boy and hundreds of others like him, then would they be any better than the people they were fighting? Would they simply replace one dictatorship with another?

Now he saw that it was this ruthlessness he distrusted in both of them. He stared back at Paul. Was the man sincere in wanting freedom or was he a malcontent opportunist who wanted power? He had taken Sheila off the streets and she seemed at least as dedicated to him as the revolution. Was that the kind of ego trip he needed? He led people like that dead boy into a dangerous confrontation and they had evidently followed him willingly enough, but Rankin wondered if Paul had actually been in the demonstration he had organized or had he been watching from a safe distance when the Sepos had opened fire on the crowd and the boy had been burned?

Rankin shoved back his chair and rose.

"Thanks for the soup. I'll be going now. "

They stared at him.

"You can spend the night, " Paul said. "We have an extra cot. "

Rankin shook his head and started for the back door. "Thanks again. "

"What about what we discussed?"

"I'll think about it."

"You'd better think quickly," Sheila said. "You've got a good chance of being caught with them swarming around out there tonight." She turned to Paul. "He might bring them down on us. I don't think you ought to let him go."

Rankin watched her narrowly. When she started to reach for her purse on the sideboard, his hand darted toward the knife.

Paul grabbed the woman's wrist. "It's up to him to do what he wants. I gave you my word, Rankin, you could stay or go." He rose from his chair and crossed to the door. He rested his hand on the knob. "There's no telephone number to call because all the lines are tapped. The only way you can get in touch with us is to come here at night. It's risky, but," he smiled tightly, "we're used to that by now. If you do, come after midnight." He unlocked the door and motioned to Sheila to turn out the light. She did and, in a moment, Rankin found himself outside in the cold darkness. The door shut behind him.

He slunk across the yard and out into the street. He cast a quick glance back at the house. It was dark like all the others and from out here any passer-by would assume its inhabitants were in bed asleep.

In the distance he could see an angry red glow. They had not been able to put out the fire. If anything, he thought, it looked bigger than before.

CHAPTER TWENTY

A persistent banging sound awoke him. He groaned, staggered up from his blanket behind the counter, and crossed to the shattered window. Outside it was still light—but a bleak, wintry gray with no sign of sun. On the abandoned house across the road a shutter flapped in the wind like a broken wing and slammed against the wall.

No one was in sight. He turned back and surveyed the interior of what had once been a country store and smiled sourly. His guts rumbled as he looked at the empty shelves around him. He had chosen the store instead of the house across the road to sleep the day away because he had wanted to be at least close to the memory of food and because he had hoped to find an old scrap of food, even a hardened rind of cheese. but there was nothing. Even the mice had apparently abandoned the place since he had seen or heard none. Anyway, he had had the snakes.

He gazed back out the window at the fading light, then went back behind the counter and began to roll up the blanket. He only traveled at night now. Winter winds had stripped the trees bare, so there was little cover from patrolling helicopters or anyone who happened to be in the woods in daytime.

So he foraged for his food at night, stealing a frozen potato left in a garden, snatching an occasional chicken from a henhouse if he could find one. He had also learned to hunt at night. He picked up the .22 automatic rifle and stroked the smooth walnut stock. it was lightweight and made little noise. He had acquired it from a redneck's pickup truck one night while the redneck was bouncing up and down on a girl on a blanket only ten yards away. Just before dawn he sometimes bagged squirrels with it and, unlike a shotgun, it did not make a mess of the meat.

But his latest food had been the snakes. Over a week ago he had found the hole in a leafy hollow, dug down into it, and discovered rattlesnakes tangled in a huge ball. They had glistened and wriggled feebly in the cold moonlight, but had been too sluggish to strike. He had eaten rattlesnake meat until yesterday morning when it had run out, and now he had to find something else.

He put the box of .22 longs into his pocket. He had gotten them from the pickup's glove compartment when he had acquired the rifle, and the box was still over half-full. Outside it was nearly dark now, and he could barely see the rolled-up blanket as he picked it up and slung it over his shoulder. The shutter still banged maddeningly in the wind. The noise drew his nerves taut. He knew he ought to wait until it was completely dark, but he was going stir-crazy in this place; he needed to get moving and find food. He looked out the window again at the lonely landscape in the dusk. There was probably not another human being within a mile, he thought. It had been three days since he had seen another person—an old man wandering across a field like some magically animated scarecrow. He had passed within a few yards of the dead weeds where Rankin had lain, and Rankin had had the crazy impulse to say something, anything to the old man just so he could hear another human voice. He had suppressed the impulse with difficulty and afterward had been overcome by a strange sadness.

How long had it been since he had talked to another human being?

The man and woman in the river town, the two revolutionists, they had been the last. He was not even sure how long ago that had been. The days and nights all seemed to blur together in a nightmare composite, and it was hard to remember now a time that he had not been on the run.

He figured it must be the middle of December now. It had been October when the man and woman—Paul and Sheila—had talked about revolution. Those were the last words Rankin had exchanged with anyone. He hardly dared talk to himself for fear his voice had disappeared.

"Damn!" he muttered. The word sounded harsh and foreign

in his ears.

It was dark outside now. With one last glance up and down the road, he stepped through the doorway into the cold wind. The shutter banged forlornly in a drum-like dirge as he started up the road.

The smell of woodsmoke grew stronger. He emerged from the trees and saw a single light across a field of rotted cotton stalks. He stopped and stared at the light for a long time. There might be a garden there he could grub in and find a ruined potato or carrot. He shivered in the wind, debating if it was worth the long trek across the field. But the longer he stared at the light, the more compelled he felt to go to it, if only to assure himself he was not alone on an empty planet whirling in a void.

The overcast had disappeared and a half moon hung in the sky. By its light, he saw as he approached, that the shack was in bad shape. The roof sagged, the brick chimney through which white smoke rose and was dissolved into wisps by the wind teetered at an odd angle, and the unpainted plank walls were badly warped.

Inside, he could make out several people crouched around the fireplace. He had a sudden impulse to knock at the door and ask if he could warm himself at their fire and simply listen to them talk.

You're going crazy, he told himself. He drew closer and peered in at the edge of the window. He counted five of them ranging from a small child to a middle-aged man and woman. The man was farthest from the fire and closest to Rankin. Rankin could see his sharp features in profile—a cheekbone that seemed to jut outside his skin and a beaked nose from which the rest of his face seemed to fall away. None of them were talking— they simply crouched or sat around the fire like dumb animals. Rankin wanted to hear them speak—if only a few muttered oaths. But none of them so much as moved—and for an eerie moment it crossed his mind that they might be dead or some wax dummies. He pressed his face closer to the dusty glass to assure himself they were real and saw another face, bearded, hollow-cheeked with dark circles beneath the eyes. For a moment he did not recognize his own reflection and when he did, it was with shock.

At the same time the man turned his head and seemed to

look directly at him.

Rankin froze. But the man's eyes had a dull, glazed look and were not focused on him at all, Rankin realized. The face seemed little more than a skull, then the man turned slowly back to the fire. Rankin studied the others more intently. They all had the same cadaverous look, and the child was bird-like with huge staring eyes in a shrivelled face.

They were starving! My God, that was why they were so listless.

He had come to steal from them and they were starving. For an instant he thought of the one-eyed mad woman whose house he had broken into and how he had stolen her meager rations.

Staring at them, he felt a curious tightness in his throat and a sensation like he had been kicked in the stomach.

He turned from the window and staggered away across the field of dead stalks. At the edge of the trees he stopped and turned once more to stare at the light. He could not rid himself of the image of the child squatting by the fire like a grotesque bird, pale and motionless.

"God!" he muttered. "My God!"

He clamped the rifle more tightly under his arm and entered the woods.

After two hours, he found and shot a horned owl that had just killed a rabbit. He slit the rabbit's belly open and pulled all the guts out in one swift motion. He headed back to the shack. By the time he reached it, the light in the window was out and so was the fire. He went to the door and knocked. He knocked again and again.

Finally after a long time he heard slow footsteps and the door opened a crack. It was the woman, bent like an old crone.

"Here, " he thrust the bloody carcasses at her. "Here! Take them!"

She stood and stared at him—not moving.

"Take them, damnit! Take them. It's food. " He thrust them inside the door at her feet, spun around on his heel, and tramped angrily across the bare yard toward the distant woods.

He came to the river. He did not know how long he had been walking, or even that he was near the river; only suddenly it was before him and he was gazing across its great width as it rolled toward the Gulf. The wind blew up whitecaps on it and stung his face until it was numb.

He sat down and rested his head in his hands. He felt numb

inside as well as outside. He had lived with fear for so long now he felt nothing. Everything he had been through since he had tried to help the school teacher that night three months ago seemed like only a vague nightmare. Even the few happy hours he had shared with Karen seemed like a dream and unreal.

And now he wandered like a sleepwalker through the nights with no plan or destination. Maybe he could go down river like he originally intended. His arm was healed now, and he could handle a boat again. As he pondered the idea, he heard a throbbing noise and lifted his head to see the lights of a towboat as it nosed a string of barges down river. He watched the tow's slow approach without bothering to conceal himself although he sat exposed on the bank in the moonlight, and it would pass probably within one hundred yards of him.

As the first two barges, in tandem, glided past, he saw two sentries on the stern of the closest hunkered down for warmth against the biting wind. They were grain barges carrying enough corn or wheat to feed thousands for weeks. He counted the other barges, a dozen in all. The waves from them lapped loudly against the bank. Then the big towboat churned abreast of him and in the lighted deckhouse he saw several well-fed men smoking and laughing. His gaze drifted up to the darkened wheelhouse for a moment; he wondered if the pilot could see him. The boat swept swiftly past. In the stern were two armed figures leaning against the rail.

He raised the rifle slowly and caught one of them in its sights. He sat with his elbows braced against his knees, the stock steady against his cheek. He took in a deep breath, let out half of it, and his finger curled more tightly against the cold trigger. Such an easy shot. He could drop the other man before the first fell to the deck.

His finger came off the trigger and he let the barrel drop. What was the point? If he killed all of them, he could still not get the grain. He needed a group—a band of men with boats could take the tow and feed the countryside. Again he saw in his mind the starving, bird-like child.

The pounding of the big diesel engines receded and the lights disappeared around a bend. Except for the whitecaps whipped up by the wind, the river was empty again.

Yes, a band of men, he thought, could have taken that tow and fed many people, including the starving family in the shack.

He might argue with the woman Sheila about whether the

people wanted freedom, but the skeletal child made his arguments now seem hollow and pointless. He did not know if Paul and Sheila really wanted a better government, a better system, but whatever they had in mind could hardly be worse than what existed now.

Some people, like the bounty hunters on the island who had shot him, and the pair of pool hall cowboys out for thrills, loved and thrived on the new way. Others, hungry and with families, might detest it, yet still feel compelled out of need to kill him or turn him in and, if Peg and Suzie were still alive and starving, would he be any different?

And yet, not everyone felt that way. Not Jason and Esther who had nursed him and given him refuge, nor Karen. She had risked her own and her son's safety to help him, and she had given him love. And somewhere in the land were more people like them—there had to be.

He thought a long time.

Finally he got up. His feet were nearly frozen, and he had to stomp around to restore circulation in them. He had to get moving.

He could go down river and try to get out of the country. Or he could head up river and try to join Paul and Sheila and fight.

He picked up the rifle and started into the woods to get away from the cutting wind off the river.

CHAPTER TWENTY-ONE

The moon above the rooftops of the drab frame houses bathed them in silvery light. It was late and the houses were dark. With the rifle wrapped in the blanket under his arm, he turned into the driveway of one of them. The shades were up in the black windows, and he sensed a heavy stillness about it.

He knocked softly on the back door through which he had departed two months earlier with a bellyful of bean soup. There was only silence within and he knocked again, harder. He peered through the kitchen window and saw faded, cracked linoleum in the moonlight, a bare table, the one with one leg shorter than the others, a bare counter, and empty sink. The kitchen had a desolate, abandoned air. He tried the window, but it was locked. So, of course, was the door.

Beside the kitchen door was another that was not locked and opened onto a small utility room. By the moonlight he made out a coiled garden hose hanging on a peg and, above it, a shelf crammed with empty flower pots, a box of plant fertilizer, and a can of spray paint. Next to the water heater was parked a beat-up power mower. A revolutionary who kept his lawn trimmed like his neighbors, Rankin thought with a small smile. Staring at these items, he felt a little let down, although Paul would hardly store hand grenades or a printing press here. He closed the door behind him and struck a match, hoping he might find something he could use on closer inspection, maybe some fishing equipment, or some .22 shells. But he found nothing else. The match flickered out, and he stood in the darkness wondering what to do. He had no idea when Paul would be back. Should he stay here and wait a while or leave and try to come back another night?

As he pondered, the door opened and his heart lurched.

He swung the rifle up still in the blanket and the figure in the doorway stepped back, her eyes enormous in the moonlight, the thin pallid face framed by red hair. It was Paul's niece, the one he had suspected of being mute.

He lowered the gun, and the girl stepped quickly inside the utility room.

"He told me to watch for you. "

So she was not a mute.

He shut the door behind her and struck another match.

"Where are they?" he said.

The girl's lips trembled. "Gone. The Sepos came and took them away. "

"When?" He felt a sinking sensation in the pit of his belly.

"Three days ago. Somebody informed on them. We don't know who. " She put her arms under her small breasts and hugged herself against the cold. "He said you would be back. He had me look out for you on nights when he was gone. I watched you come in here from my bedroom window. "

"What's happened to them—do you know?"

Her big eyes swam for an instant. "I don't know. They say he and Sheila are enemies of the state—like you, " she whispered. "We've heard they are already dead, but we don't know. "

The match burned his fingers and died. He did not bother to light another one.

"Have you got anything to eat?" she said. "They've cut our rations."

"No. What do you mean, cut rations? Why?"

"There have been more riots—all over, Uncle Paul said. So they cut our food—to punish us and bring us back in line, he said. "

He thought again of the family he had seen in the shack two nights ago.

"How long has it been?"

"I don't know. Right after Thanksgiving. Nearly a month. "

They stood silent in the blackness. Rankin's mind whirled. Since making his decision two nights ago on the river bank, he had counted on joining with Paul's group. Sheila had been right. Alone he could accomplish little. A group could have perhaps taken that big tow of grain barges, and people like the family in the shack and the girl beside him would not be starving. But somewhere in other places would be other groups. Paul had said an underground network was springing up all over the country.

Somehow he had to make contact with them. Maybe there were even members of Paul's group who were still free and still ready to fight if only he could find them.

"Haven't you got any food?" the girl asked. "Anything?"

"I'm sorry. I've got nothing. "

"You have a gun. You can shoot something to eat. Take me with you. " An eagerness crept into her voice. "Please. "

"I can't. "

"Yes, you can. You can!" she whispered. "You know you can. " Suddenly he felt her press against him. "I'm older than I look. I'm almost sixteen. I can give you what you need. How long has it been for you? I bet a long time. Hasn't it?"

"Don't, " he rasped. "Don't you think if I had anything, I'd let you have some? But I don't. I haven't eaten in three days. Do you know what kind of life it is out there—on the run?"

"I don't care!" she said. "It can't be any worse than this. " A long, wrenching sob broke from her throat.

He put his arms around her and felt her thin, bony shoulder blades. She shuddered and he felt her hot tears against his cheek. He held her until the sobbing stopped.

"What can we do?" she said at last.

"I wish I knew. " He released her. "Do you know anyone else in town who worked with your uncle?"

"No. He never told me. He said I was too young to get involved. " She gave a bitter laugh. "But I'm not too young to starve. " Her voice became suddenly hard. "I won't. And I'm going to fight those bastards. I'm going to fight them. I'll do anything I have to do to survive. Anything! My mother and I won't starve. I won't let us! And one day they'll pay!"

"Yes. " He did not know whether he believed it or not. But he admired her resiliency. A minute ago she had seemed utterly defeated in his arms, but the tears had been a necessary release. He wondered how long she had held them in; at any rate, she had the strength of youth going for her, and that was something.

He squeezed her arm. "I've got to go. And your mother is probably worried about you. " He cracked the door and looked outside. Nothing stirred in the chill moonlight. "Go on, " he said.

She stared at him a moment longer. "I hope you'll be all right. " Then she brushed past him and was gone. He wanted to wish her luck, but the words stuck in his throat. He felt like a weight was pressing against his chest.

Glumly he surveyed again the contents of the utility room, his mind on the girl. I'm going to fight them! she had said. She was Paul's niece, all right. He wondered if she would make it through the winter.

The moonlight gleamed on the can of spray paint on the shelf. He picked it up idly and shook it. He wondered how long ago Paul or Sheila had bought it. Whatever they had bought it for, they would never be using it again. He pushed on the nozzle and a thin jet of paint spurted onto the wall. He stared at it dully. He could not have taken the girl with him; it would have endangered both of them more. At least here she still had a ration card that insured her of some food anyway. Still, the thought that she might not make it through the winter persisted. And yet what could he do about it? Nothing. His hand clamped tightly on the spray can in anger and frustration.

He remembered the books Karen had given him, the books by Chekhov and Solzhenitsyn. Solzhenitsyn had fought with the only weapon he had—and so had the school teacher, Samuel Ross. Rankin remembered thinking what an idiot Ross had been to nail up a stupid document. It had cost him his life. Now he realized it had been the only real weapon Ross could muster, ineffectual though it had been. In the end, you had to fight them whatever way you could, he thought. Whatever way you could with whatever was at hand. And if you did not, you might as well be dead anyway, because you already were—inside.

He crossed the street, followed an alley and came to another empty, poorly-lit street. Then he saw what he was looking for, the pawnshop and beyond it the entrance to the alley. He reached the alley and stared at the spot where the boy had lain with the laser hole through his guts. Finally, he gazed at the clammy brick wall next to it.

He pressed down on the nozzle of the paint can and made one long vertical streak, then a short horizontal one across it. The cross was blood-red.

He stood back and looked at it. In daylight people would see it fine—and they would know. He looked up at the sky. In a couple more hours it would be dawn and he would have to be out of town by then or else find a good hiding place. He started up the street and ahead, at a cross street, saw a windowless stucco wall and on it a large poster. As he drew closer, he read the bold black letters:

THE
SECURITY POLICE
PROTECT YOU!

He crossed the street to the poster and looked furtively around.

With the spray can he crossed out the word "PROTECT" and started to substitute a word in its place. But suddenly he had another idea. He ripped down the poster and tore it to pieces. The breeze blew the pieces into the street. Then he started forming letters on the blank wall.

So intent was he on what he was doing that he failed to notice the car gliding almost silently down the street until almost the last moment. As he finished and stepped back, he heard the car, turned, and saw one of the Sepos rolling down the window with a laser in his hand.

He dropped the spray can and slipped the rifle free from the blanket. The car stopped, and Rankin sprinted across the street. He heard the car door open and a yell. He flung a quick glance behind him, glimpsed the man leveling the laser at him in front of blood-like letters a foot high:

THE
SECURITY POLICE
DESTROY YOU

He rounded the corner and a spray of brick chips stung the back of his neck. A car door slammed and tires squealed. He turned up a side street and ran as hard as he could, looked back once, and saw the cruiser round the corner. He was running up an incline and his lungs burned.

Behind him the roar of the car's engine drowned out the blood hammering in his ears. He ran past a warehouse, topped the crest of the hill, and saw below him only fifty yards away the river.

Without pausing he dashed toward the bank. He saw no boat

and he knew the water would be icy, and that he was too weak from the run and hunger to try and fight the strong current. He stopped at the edge of the bank.

Turning, he felt the cold wind stab at his back, saw the twin beams of the headlights shoot up over the hill. Then he swung the rifle up to meet them. He was no longer an Enemy of the State. They were.